PARADIGM SHIFT

Andrew Srour

Paradigm Shift
First published in Australia by Andrew Srour 2020

Copyright © Andrew Srour 2020
All Rights Reserved

 A catalogue record for this book is available from the National Library of Australia

ISBN: 978-0-6488579-0-7 (pbk)
ISBN: 978-0-6488579-1-4 (ebk)

Typesetting and design by Publicious Book Publishing
Published in collaboration with Publicious Book Publishing
www.publicious.com.au

Cover image: © agungsptr

All characters and events in this publication are fictitious, any resemblance to real persons, living or dead, or any events past or present are purely coincidental.

No part of this book may be reproduced in any form, by photocopying or by any electronic or mechanical means, including information storage or retrieval systems, without permission in writing from both the copyright owner and the publisher of this book.

Contents

Chapter 1: The Crash 1

Chapter 2: The Hospital 4

Chapter 3: Perspective 12

Chapter 4: Discharged 30

Chapter 5: Confrontation 41

Chapter 6: Roots 59

Chapter 7: The Rundown 70

Chapter 8: Moments 87

Chapter 9: Two Families in Four Nights 102

Chapter 10: The Talk 117

Chapter 11: Sticking to the Plan 125

Chapter 12: First Trimester 137

Chapter 13: Burning Out 146

Chapter 14: Exchange for a Miracle 155

Chapter 15: A Different Kind of Shower 163

Chapter 16: Weekend of a Lifetime 171

Chapter 17: Persistent, Resilient, Eager 183

Chapter 18/Epilogue: Adjusting 195

CHAPTER 1

The Crash

Currently, I'm sitting in the hospital recovering, but let me explain exactly what happened.

It was a Friday morning, around 8:30am. The sun was fresh in the sky, warming up the day while I was driving to work. I started my day as I usually do. I got into my car, connected my phone to the speakers and played my music, with the windows down. The music was a little louder than it should have been, which might have interfered with my hearing, but that wasn't cause of the accident.

About 15 minutes after driving the back streets, I ended up back on a main road. My phone buzzed. I was stopped at a red light.

People always say not to use your phone while you're driving. We've all heard the stories; some of us may have even experienced them firsthand. Those heartbreaking last messages that read, 'See you soon' or 'On my way'. Those horrific advertisements that are meant to discourage drivers from using their phones in the car, the statistics, the lives lost.

Unfortunately, living in the modern world, we're all glued to our phones. The temptation to check your phone in the car is killer, or at least it can be. We've all done it. It doesn't always lead to the worst case scenario. If I'm being honest, I usually would check my phone while driving. However on this day I was enjoying my music too much to reply to my friends, and I wasn't too far from my destination.

So, I flipped my phone face down, ignoring the messages and the vibrations that followed them. Thankfully I'm not always too attached to my phone. Disregarding my phone entirely, I continued belting out the lyrics of my music, which sometimes can be just as dangerous as checking your phone, when you're getting really into it. The neighbouring drivers always stare at me, but that will never stop me from doing my thing.

The lights turned green and I stepped on the accelerator. I've been told I have a heavy foot. When I turned my head, I saw the car coming straight for me, but I couldn't do anything. It felt like I was in the movies, with my whole life flashing before my eyes. However, it was just the speed camera flashing the other car. I don't know how fast the other car was going but I remember the sound as the vehicle came into collision with mine, the loud crash, the screeching and crunching of metal, the glass shattering, the sound of my car flipping over. It flipped four times, I was informed later. At some point during the contact I hit my head, and then I didn't remember much at all.

I was in and out of consciousness on the way to the hospital. I have zero recollection of being pulled out of the car or being put into the ambulance, but I remember there was a lot of noise from the sirens and a lot of light every time I managed to peak through my eyelids. The bumps in the road made my eyes open and then I was in the stretcher in the ambulance. I tried to ask where I was and what happened, but nothing came out.

Before I knew it, I felt my head pulsing and ringing. A wave of pain came from all over my body and my mouth made a noise, but words were not what escaped.

CHAPTER 2

The Hospital

The next thing I know, I'm lying in a hospital bed. Before I could open my eyes and see where I was, my ears adjusted, and I could hear everything. There was a conversation happening outside, machines and monitors beeping and buzzing. My eyes felt sealed shut; they didn't seem to want to open. I absorbed whatever I could of what was happening around me, using the senses that I could use.

Someone was reading my chart to another person, possibly a nurse, and the voice that I heard was beautifully soft and soothing, almost enchanting.

'The patient has been vocally unresponsive, but we have his identification from his wallet. His driver's license says that his name is Jacob Bartelli and he's 24 years old. He was involved in a car accident on one of the intersections on the main road. Currently suffering from a concussion, he also has major bruising throughout most of his upper and lower body. There may be potential internal injuries, possible fractures or broken ribs, and he has a fractured left leg. There was an open gash on the right hip but that has been treated and is healing. The skull is intact and there should be no additional head trauma. Once the patient is awake and responsive, we will be able to conduct further tests to confirm any additional injuries. If the patient is still not conscious after an hour, page Doctor Martinez and ask him to have the tests done as soon as possible. For now, keep an eye out for any irregularities, and if there are any changes make sure and let me know, understood?'

'Yes, Doctor Abrahms.'

'Also, try to find a contact, a family member or friend. I'll be in the room doing a scan if you need to page me.'

Doctor Abrahms was her name, and she was definitely not a nurse. Her voice was powerful, soothing to my ears, she had a tone of confidence and assurance. In a failed attempt to wake, I drifted back into sleep.

I woke up briefly and had a chance to put the face to the voice. Doctor Abrahms was there in front of my eyes. At least I thought it was the same person.

'Your husband is a lucky man,' I mumbled. I was groggy, and I don't recall myself saying that aloud but before I dozed back to sleep, I heard her chuckle.

'Damn right he is,' she said.

I don't know how long it was before I woke up, but it felt as though a lifetime had come and gone. When I finally managed to open my eyes, the bright lights were the first thing that pierced through. Maybe it had been a lifetime. It was clearly morning and the sunlight glared through the windows. The second thing I noticed were the casts and bandages on my body. My leg had a cast and was slightly raised, and my left arm and chest were connected and wrapped in a cast. My body felt so stiff and it was uncomfortable and I just wanted to stretch.

The third thing I saw, or rather didn't see, was the absence of a nurse or a doctor.

I was alone in the room adjusting to everything. It was only about three minutes before the pain shot rapidly through my chest. I couldn't help myself from screaming in agony.

I tried to feel around for a button, whether a button for calling a nurse or morphine I don't know, but I couldn't even focus on that. Almost within seconds of my uncontrollable screams, a male figure wearing blue scrubs came running into my room and found the morphine button for me. I think I must have been hyperventilating because the man, who only looked a little older than me, began to help me to take deep, heavy breaths, which calmed me down. The monitor started to ease up on its beeping as my breathing fell into a steady rhythm. I could feel the drops of sweat flowing down my head.

When I calmed down and grew aware of my surroundings again, I realised that the man, a nurse as it turned out, was absolutely stunning. He had green sparkling eyes that pierced into me, beautiful dark brown hair, a cute yet cheeky smirk framed with a slight stubbled beard and a fit, toned body. I felt paralysed, and it wasn't because of the accident. I don't know if it was the morphine or if I was just mesmerised.

'Are one of the requirements of working here being drop dead gorgeous'?' I asked.

I quickly realised I'd spoken aloud and instinctively tried to cover my mouth with my hand. But I was stopped by my cast, which then forced a slight yelp of pain out of my mouth. I felt myself blushing and apologised for what I had said.

The nurse, named Nathaniel, he said, burst into laughter. Then he blushed a little and picked up his chart

'Thank you, I'm extremely flattered,' he said. 'But wouldn't you like to know about your condition and what happened to you?'.

I was a little confused, 'Yeah, I guess so. I know I was in a car accident. Did anything happen after that?' I tried to pay attention but all I could concentrate on was his eyes; they drew me in. My eyes then dropped and I focused on his lips. As they opened, the soothing voice that followed allowed the details to flow out.

'Yes, you did have a pretty horrific car accident, resulting in your injuries. You've suffered bruising almost entirely across your body, your left leg is in fact broken and two of your ribs on the left side of your torso are fractured. Your right shoulder is also slightly fractured but should be the first to recover. Scans were taken and didn't show any signs of internal bleeding. Your head, apart from the concussion suffered after the accident, was declared uninjured, but you may experience a strong headache when your body starts to recover.'

I may have been slightly distracted, and it took me a moment to soak in everything that Nathaniel was saying. I froze for a while. Nathaniel didn't move or say anything. But the silence was soon shattered.

'Are you all right Mr Bartelli?' he asked. 'I know it's a lot to take in.'

'Yeah, I'm alright I just... I guess I'm just really lucky. I don't even really remember what happened, it was all so fast. Also, please just call me Jacob. Did you by any chance know what happened with the other driver? Do you know why they were speeding?' I wasn't sure whether to feel angry at the other driver or to just be grateful to be alive.

'I'm not too sure about the other driver, but I can try find out for you Mr Bartelli, sorry, Jacob. We also couldn't get a hold of your parents or any family members, was there anybody that we could call for you?' he asked.

'Thank you. My parents left recently on holiday for three weeks, please don't ring them. I don't want to worry them and make them come back early or anything.'

I noticed Nathaniel clench his fist as he listened. He seemed to be a little on edge.

'So, you're going to be all by yourself? Do you have anybody you could call?'

It seemed as though he was frustrated or worried that I was all alone, so I lied.

'I have a friend I can call.' It wasn't a total lie. I do have friends that I could call, but I just wasn't in the mood for anyone's company right then. I just needed some time to myself. 'I just need to let work know what happened, and I don't know where my phone is.'

Nathaniel's tension eased a little 'Your work called earlier, and I answered your phone, sorry. I informed them of what happened, and they were very compassionate. They wish you the best. Here's your phone, it was, surprisingly, unscathed.'

As he passed me my phone, my hands were shaking. I think it was too heavy for me with all my injuries. I dropped the phone into my lap so that I didn't drop it anywhere else.

'Did you put your number in there?' I jokingly asked, but before Nathaniel could get a word in, Doctor Abrahms entered the room.

'Mr Bartelli how are you feeling?' she said. As I looked up her eyes bored into me, a glowing, calming blue. Her wavy, silky light-brown hair fell just below her shoulders. She was simply gorgeous. She had very defined cheekbones, and her presence alone just exuded confidence.

'The other drop-dead gorgeous doctor,' I whispered aloud. Instinctively I gave her a smile and attempted a wink, to which she responded with a glare.

'The other?' she responded and winked back at me. 'You do remember that I have my damn lucky husband? I can't say the same for Nathaniel though…' she went on. Nathaniel was confused at first, then his eyes widened, his cheeks grew a bright red and he smirked with his lips.

'I'll be right back,' he said, quickly stepping out of the room.

Doctor Abrahms giggled as soon as Nathaniel fled the room.

'He can be such a nervous wreck sometimes, but he makes a great nurse. Young blood. Speaking of that, your heart rate seems to be a lot steadier. It's slightly elevated but much better. Now I need to discuss a few things with you Mr Bartelli. Firstly, your car was totalled during the accident, so you will have to call up your insurance company and sort out the details so you can be compensated, both for the car and the medical fees. If you need assistance getting home, we can organise a taxi, but we'll focus on that when the time comes.'

'Thank you, Doctor, do you know how long I'll be kept here for?'

'Most likely for another two weeks, depending on how stable you are and how quick your recovery is. It might take a few extra days or so, since we have a few extra beds and you're alone, it might be better if you stay. Did Nurse Nathaniel not call anybody for you?'

I told Doctor Abrahms about my family being on holiday and that I could call a friend if I needed to.

'Do it' Doctor Abrahms sighed. 'Don't be too stubborn to ask help from those close to you. You will be on crutches for a while after you're discharged, and it might take a little while before you're back on your feet again. Even while you're in here, we're going to have to get you used to the crutches before you leave. If you're lucky, you might not even be here for two weeks.'

'Hmm, two weeks with Nurse Nathaniel?' I thought to myself out loud. At that, Doctor Abrahms let out a slight laugh and smirked at me.

'Well honestly, I'm not too sure about his schedule, but he'll be here, as will others. Please don't give him a hard time, he's like a son to me and he's recently had a tough breakup with his boyfriend.'

'So, he *is* gay!' I knew it, I just had a feeling. I couldn't contain my smile. But in the next moment, there was a feeling of pain that started to return. It was a little less intense, but the rush was still agonising. Enough for me to reach over and press the button for my dose of morphine.

Doctor Abrahms was on her way out.

'Do you know anything about the other car?' I remembered to ask her. 'I asked Nathaniel, but he didn't know anything. I just want to know why they ran the red light. Did something happen? Why did they hit me?' I realised at that point that I was raising my voice a little bit; I didn't mean to get worked up. I felt warm, wet tears trickle down my face.

'I'm sorry Mr Bartelli, I'll have Nurse Nathaniel try to find out for you, but I haven't heard anything about the other car. I know you're in pain but try to get some rest.' Doctor Abrahms gave me a faint smile on her way out.

I couldn't hold back the tears anymore. They just kept flowing down my face. I was glad that I was alone in the room. Everything hit me, again. I was overwhelmed from the pain, the shock, the silence, the cast, the car, from so many things to deal with. My eyes started to close down as did the walls around me. I wiped the tears off my face for the night before drifting off to sleep.

CHAPTER 3

Perspective

I could feel the saliva dried up around my mouth. My lips were dry, cracking, and sore. Habitually I grabbed my phone and my reflection in the screen wasn't very appealing, and I felt withered. My throat was aching for water, a thirst that needed to be quenched instantly. I wasn't so sure when it had arrived, but there was a bottle of water on the side of my bed along with a banana and a small tub of jelly. Stretching out my free hand, I grasped the bottle and pulled it into my lap to open it. I awkwardly lifted it to my lips, gulping mouthfuls of water, allowing the lukewarm water to bring a bit of life and satisfaction to my body, both inside and out, as I managed to drink some water.

How did people brush their teeth in here? I mean, obviously, I knew how, but how was I supposed to do that when I couldn't get out of bed? Was I meant to ask the nurse, or should I just not brush my teeth? I supposed at this moment it wasn't the *most* important thing, but I still wanted to, I felt dirty and unhygienic.

It was almost 11 in the morning and I still hadn't seen a nurse for a while, so I pressed the button to call for one. I hated being impatient, and I didn't want to be rude. If it wasn't an emergency I felt like there was no need for me to call, but I was intent on brushing my teeth, and I was starting to feel lonely…

A nurse came in, another male. It wasn't Nathaniel. I asked about the whole toothbrush situation and it turned out I had to do it in bed and then had to rinse out afterwards into a cup. I felt disgusting but it had to be done. I just wanted to have a shower and clean up.

I just can't wait to get out of here, I thought. I wonder if I can even shower here or if it is just like a sponge bath, or what if I need to pee. Fuck! Now I need to pee…

I'll spare you the details but it's safe to say that I needed help. The pain from getting up was excruciating at first, but it soon became bearable. I'll be able to slow down on the morphine for now, I thought. It will still be another day or two before I'd be able to try walking with the crutches on my own. In the meantime, I was supposed to rest, and it wasn't like I could really do anything else.

So I'm stuck in the room watching boring daytime television shows, I can't read a book with one arm and even so I haven't even got any books with me. I supposed I could call someone to come and visit but I decided not to tell anybody. The nurse has been in and out of my room, I think he's busy, so he doesn't really talk much, just checks up on me. I don't blame him.

By now it was almost 3pm and I had done nothing all day but attempt to watch TV while falling in and out of sleep. At some point during my awakenings, I saw Nathaniel swap out with the other nurse. When he came to check up on me, he had a serious look on his face, so I tried to cheer him up.

'I guess not all the staff here pass the 'gorgeous' criteria' I said, indicating the other nurse who'd just left with my eyes. I felt like I might have been too cruel. 'I'm only kidding,' I said.

It broke his seriousness for a moment. He released a slight giggle, but only for a moment. Then the seriousness returned on his face. I got lost looking into his eyes, unintentionally, then I realised that maybe I was too hasty with my comment. I didn't want to offend him. 'I'm sorry if that was rude and if I've been a jerk. I don't want to make work a bother for you or anything like that. Doctor Abrahms mentioned something about your ex-boyfriend so I guess I was just trying to lighten the mood.'

His face crinkled, 'She said what? Uh, it doesn't matter, that's not the issue, I just need to talk to you about something and it's quite intense.'

'You're right, I'm sorry.' I felt guilty and embarrassed.

'No, I'm flattered honestly, but it's just… that's not what this is about. Mr Bartelli, it's about the other car. I tried to sort out the insurance for you and in doing so I learned all the details, that the other driver was in this hospital in the other ward, but that she didn't make it.'

'Oh… wow.' I put my head down into my hands and started crying. I just couldn't help it. I knew it wasn't my fault and that I couldn't have done anything about what happened, but I felt responsible for the other driver's life. There was a wave of emotion that just took over me. I didn't know how old she was or why she was speeding, if she left behind a family or if she was alone in the car. I couldn't ask Nathaniel; I couldn't speak. I just needed a moment to let myself break down before I could manage to build up to it.

It took a while for me to slow down my tears. Nathaniel began comforting me with his arms, hugging and consoling me. He then sat next to me after I had calmed down a little bit.

'There's more that I need to discuss with you regarding the family,' he said.

I felt so confused, like a platform beneath me had vanished into thin air and I was falling with no landing place in sight. Was I a bad person because I was so angry at the other driver? At a person who didn't survive and has potentially left behind a family?

'What do you mean? What else is there?'

'I need to tell you why the other driver was speeding. Usually I'm not supposed to, however the other family has requested that you know.' Nathaniel sounded extremely sincere.

I was overwhelmed and perplexed. I couldn't understand why the family would want me to know what had happened. Maybe they just didn't want me to be angry with the driver. I guess knowing what happened and why will help to give me a sense of closure.

At that moment, Nathaniel took a deep breath, looked into my eyes, and grabbed one of my hands with both of his. My heart was racing, beating fast with fear and curiosity. I don't know if he meant this to be comforting, but I wasn't complaining.

'The other driver was an elderly woman. You probably didn't see her when she crashed into you, but she couldn't stop because she was having a heart attack while driving. There's a possibility that it made her fall in and out of consciousness. After the crash, she was rushed here to the hospital, but she didn't make it. Her heart didn't recover and she was pronounced dead moments after she arrived.'

My body was shaking, and I couldn't steady myself. Even the hand that Nathaniel was holding was violently trembling and my body was tense all over. I didn't think for a moment that the other driver was anything other than reckless, only to learn that they had been suffering too. I could feel my eyes welling up and more tears were starting to form.

I didn't want Nathaniel to see me break down, but as I tried to speak to ask him to leave my voice cracked before I could get any words out. I reached for my pillow to cover my face and started sobbing aggressively into it. I was angry, then upset and then guilty. My emotions were scattered, and I just couldn't take it anymore. I had literally cried three times in the last two days. I had no idea why I was such a mess!

A warm, comforting hand was rubbing my back, stabilising the beat of my heart. I had almost forgotten that he was there. He took the pillow from my hand, revealing my face, which probably looked like a mess. He looked into my eyes, gave me a small smile, and hugged me. I didn't know he was allowed to do that, but I guess sometimes that could be more helpful than the medicine.

The past couple of days had been a strange whirlwind.

Minutes passed by before I stopped crying and calmed myself down. When I finally did, Nathaniel started to speak again.

'Mr Bartelli…'

'Jacob' I mumbled, correcting him.

'Jacob.' He repeated back to me. There was a long, sickening pause in which I braced for whatever was about to flow out of his mouth. 'There's one more thing that I need to tell you, about the other family. This might seem a little strange, but the son and daughter of the driver would like to meet with you. They are both adults and they requested that I ask you. They want to talk to you and apologise on behalf of their mother. They insisted that I asked you to set up a meeting.'

'No!' I refused instantly. 'They have nothing to apologise for and there's no reason why they should want to speak to me. I don't see the point.' I didn't realise that my voice had gotten louder and more aggressive.

'Jacob!' Nathaniel's voice rose too and it startled me. He was stern and I didn't think his mind was going to change. 'You haven't had any visitors since you got here, I know for a fact that you didn't call your friend and I know you don't want to bother your parents so why not meet up with this family. What have you got to lose?'

My face was red with embarrassment about not calling a friend. I didn't know what to say, but Nathaniel did.

'It might even help you understand that this wasn't your fault and if it doesn't help you then at least it might help them grieve a little; and it would make me worry a little less.'

Nathaniel's face was burning up, I could see the passion and intensity rise in his body. But why would he be worrying? I didn't realise that nurses cared that much, I was being stubborn.

'Fine, you're right. I'll speak with them, if it will somehow help them with this entire situation then I guess I can't really not meet them.' I conceded.

A smile bloomed on Nathaniel's face. 'Great, I'll go talk to them and bring them in.'

'Wait, they're already here? What if I didn't say yes?' I asked, feeling slightly manipulated.

'They had to come back to deal with some paperwork, plus I knew I'd be able to persuade you with my charm.'

He winked before leaving the room.

Meeting the family was a strange yet fulfilling experience. The children, Bryan and Jennifer, looked several years older than me. They apologised multiple times, but I assured them each time that it was an unfortunate accident and that there was nothing they needed to apologise for. They spoke to me about their mother, Judith, who had been suffering from a heart condition over the last couple of years. They talked to me about her life and related some of the memories that they shared about her.

They mentioned that Judith's husband, their father, had also passed away almost three years ago and that Judith hadn't been the same since. She had lived a full life and regardless of what happened, her family was always her pride and joy. Judith had been 74 years old and her children adored her very much. They always would. They spoke very highly of their mother, and somehow didn't have any resentment towards me.

I knew that the accident wasn't my fault, but I still expected some sort of anger. But they were both such sweet, kind and caring people. Tears were shared between the three of us and it made me realise how helpful it had been for me to talk to them, to talk to someone. I could only hope that they experienced a similar outcome from talking to me.

They seemed to be happy, despite everything that had happened. The circumstances were difficult to process, however Bryan and Jennifer both said that they knew Judith's soul was at peace now, with their father. By the end of the conversation, we were all drained and I was exhausted.

I thanked Nathaniel after they left, and he smiled at me, before going home. It had been an emotional day and I knew that I needed to rest, so I did I. I let my body shut itself down and I slept.

A week had passed, a week of lying in bed, eating underwhelming hospital food. It wasn't the worst but I had just been craving something junky, McDonalds or a pepperoni pizza. But Doctor Abrahms said to try and hold off for a little bit; I don't know why. Her voice was so soothing though that I always listened to what she said no matter what.

The television programs had been rather boring. Daytime shows are not always that entertaining, especially when you've been watching them for a week. Although, there had been a few decent movies on throughout the week. As for Nathaniel, I hadn't seen him since that day after meeting with Judith's family. The nurse said today that my cast would be coming off on my arm, and that, that while my ribs were still healing, I'd be able to use the crutches to walk. I supposed I should get used to being alone for a while.

It was around noon when Doctor Abrahms and the nurse came back into the room. This time the nurse was a sturdy and beautiful African American lady with flawless skin. I tried to lift myself up, with help from the nurse, to get ready for Doctor Abrahms to cut the cast. The electric saw they used look extremely frightening and I had to hold my breath for a moment while she cut into the cast. The loud whirring sound that the saw made was terrifying and it was hard to watch but it was obvious that she knew what she was doing.

Doctor Abrahms removed the cast from my arm as well as the bandaging around my ribs. I still had to keep cast for my leg for quite some time. The skin underneath the cast was slightly discoloured compared to the rest of my body. It was shower time. My arm would be fine to use, but Doctor Abrahms wanted to keep my ribs in a tight bandage wrap afterwards just to be safe.

The shower was a little painful and a slightly awkward but it was refreshing at the same time. Doctor Abrahms made sure to wrap my chest afterwards and then told me it might be better to wait until tonight, when I could try and walk with the crutches with Nathaniel's help.

I thought about it for a moment, but I couldn't wait any longer. I was too eager to try because I had been stuck in the bed for too long. So, the nurse and Doctor Abrahms handed me the crutches and helped me get off the bed.

At first, it was painful, not excruciating but irritating and uncomfortable. My arm was not as strong or as stable as it used to be, and it was difficult to support my body. The goal was to walk down the hallway and then come back, but I had to take it easy for now.

The pain eased a little after I had gotten from the room to the hall, but it was weird adjusting to the crutches. I had to balance my weight and create a rhythm with my movements, figuring out how to maintain my motions with each step. I almost lost my balance turning into the hallway, however I managed to stay upright. It took a moment to get into it but then I started heading down the hallway and I was determined to get to the goal.

I was walking slowly but I eventually made my way to the end. It was a tad uncomfortable to turn back around but I took my time and shifted my body. Coming back was much easier than taking off and before I knew it, I was back on my bed.

I have to admit, when I laid back down on the bed I was out of breath. My arms were sore, and I could feel the exhaustion coming, but Doctor Abrahms was very proud and that made me feel good. It was strange to think that I'd be going home soon. I felt like I'd been here for so long, but it had been barely a week.

I don't remember when I fell asleep or how long I fell asleep for, but suddenly I was being woken up by Doctor Abrahms.

'Wake up Mr Bartelli, I have a surprise for you!' she whispered with a bundle of enthusiasm. It was a little too much excitement for me after just waking up. 'I won't be able to enjoy it with you because I have to go. It was supposed to be for later on, as a reward for walking with the crutches, but since you already started…' She smiled and then left the room. I had no idea what the surprise was, but I waited patiently, forcing myself to be up and awake.

Before I knew it, Nathaniel walked in with a box of something. He had a big, goofy smile on his face. Then I looked at the box and noticed that it was a box of pizza! He sat next to me, opened the box, and the smell of pepperoni and cheese gave the room a fresh new aroma.

'Doctor Abrahms said you were asking for this the other day, then asked me to get it today as a reward! I heard that your walk with the crutches went quite well.

How did you feel? I know they're a little uncomfortable at first, but you'll get used to them in no time, and it's not permanent, thankfully.'

I couldn't help myself, the tears just started flowing down my cheeks. I was so overwhelmed with how much effort they had put in for me. I was overcome with emotion. Nathaniel's eyes widened in surprise, shock and worry.

'Hey! Mr Bartelli… Jacob, what's wrong?' He sounded concerned.

I had to wipe my tears and sniff my nose. 'I just… I don't understand it. I don't understand why you and Doctor Abrahms are so nice to me. You guys care so much and I never… I never expected anything like this. It's been so draining and stressful and scary, this entire week, and I just don't know how to thank you both. I'm sorry for being such a mess. Aren't there other patients who need your attention?' I finished.

Nathaniel said that it was nice and quiet this week. Then he opened the box of pizza and passed me a slice.

I noticed his face contort with a strange smirk; I don't think he expected such an overdramatic response from me. He hugged me and I could instantly feel the warmth passing onto me from his toned arms. Then he laughed at me, telling me not to worry about thanking him or Doctor Abrahms for doing their jobs. Then he grabbed a slice of pizza for himself while I wiped the rest of my tears away and tried to lighten up the mood.

Several moments later, my phone rang, Mum was calling.

My family still didn't know anything, and I had no intention of telling them any time soon, not until they came back from their holiday. My mother, father and brother had gone to Lebanon to visit some relatives and then they were heading to Italy to see Dad's parents.

Nathaniel gave me a calculating look after I ignored the call and put the phone down.

'I'll call her back later,' I said. Then I asked Nathaniel what the problem was, but I already knew what had upset him. He said he didn't want me to be alone.

'So, are you going to show me?' he asked.

I looked down at my waist and then back up to Nathaniel.

'Umm, don't you think it's a little early for that? I also don't think this is the most appropriate place to just 'show you', and I think I'd rather be clean for whenever that time comes.' I knew that wasn't what he meant but I had no clue what he was talking about.

'Oh God, no!' He rolled his eyes and then sighed. He blushed a little but then he explained what he'd meant.

'I mean, are you going to show me how you use the crutches? Are you up for taking a walk? You need a little more practice before you leave.'

I didn't know that I had the energy to do so, but I guessed Nathaniel was right. I needed to get used to walking with them at some point, so I grabbed the crutches and got up.

Once again focusing on the rhythm and the pace of my steps, I was comfortable moving, and I felt like I was a lot steadier than I was the first time. It felt weird taking steps with the crutches, but I thought I was doing quite well. Then, unexpectedly, a pain jolted up into my arm. There was a cramp coming and my muscle froze up. I jerked my arm and dropped the crutches, trying to shift myself and lean on the wall, but Nathaniel ran over to catch me before I could fall.

'I'm sorry, it just started cramping and it was hurting.' I could hear the anger and frustration in my voice. I just wanted to cry but I'd already done that so many times.

'Hey, it's fine, I'm sorry for pushing you but you did really well, you should be proud. It will be second nature to you in no time. Let's just wait until your cramp goes away and then we can make our way back to the room for some more pizza.' And so, we did, we just stood there, me in my hospital gown with the cramp in my arm pulsing while he was holding me up. I was leaning against the wall. I looked down and felt it before I saw it. My genitalia had received too much blood flow than I ever anticipated in this moment.

'Oh, um, can we try walking back now please?'

Nathaniel gave me a puzzled look and then he tried to help me. He directed his eyes down to grab the crutches and then he saw what I was looking at, hoping he wouldn't see. He let out a little giggle and I could feel my entire face flare with embarrassment.

'It's been a while, Okay! I didn't want to do anything while I was in the hospital! It's the cramp I swear, it's messing around with my blood flow.' I couldn't stop stuttering, fuck, this was too embarrassing.

'Mmm' he giggled as he blushed. 'You do realise I am a nurse, right? But sure, let's blame the 'blood flow' on the cramp.' He winked and laughed some more.

At that, I cringed way too much, but my cramp was subsiding. I turned around away from Nathaniel and decided to hop my way back to my bed.

'Hey, wait!' he exclaimed. I heard him pick up the crutches, but I was already headed towards the room.

I made my way back into my bed and I quickly grabbed my pillow and covered my face to hide it. I heard Nathaniel step in with the crutches.

'You can leave me now and let my embarrassment eat me alive.' I announced in a muffled voice.

He started laughing at me. He grabbed the pillow from my face and told me it was fine, that's he'd seen much worse in this place.

'Plus, I wasn't complaining.' He said. He winked at me before leaving the room. 'Get some rest, we need to talk tomorrow. Goodnight and sweet dreams!' He threw another wink my way and walked out of the room.

It seemed like Nathaniel was giving me some sort of vibe, like he was flirting back at me. Maybe I was just delusional; I was also too exhausted to care at this point. The smell of pizza in the room still lingered and it helped ease me to sleep.

For the first time since being at the hospital, I had an easy, peaceful sleep. When I woke up, I surprisingly wasn't in much pain, only my head felt heavy. Doctor Abrahms walked into the room not long after.

'Good morning Mr Bartelli, did you enjoy your pizza?' She was always so bubbly, no matter the time of the day.

'Yes, I did. Thank you so much Doctor Abrahms! I don't know how to tha...'

'It's fine!' Doctor Abrahms interrupted. 'Nurse Nathaniel told me everything that happened, about how you were feeling and that you went for a walk. I heard you got an unexpected cramp, amongst other things.' Doctor Abrahms winked and then laughed in a cruel manner.

I felt my face blush but I returned the laughter.

'Not to worry, it is something that happens to many patients. The stress on the body sometimes causes that reaction.' She smiled and sounded extremely reassuring in her dictation.

I was waiting for Nathaniel to come see me. I remember he said that he had something to talk about. It was starting to make me feel anxious and worried.

'Doctor Abrahms, do you know where Nathaniel is by any chance? He said yesterday that he needed to talk about something, and it's been eating at me.'

'He'll be here soon. He wanted to talk to you about when you'll be discharged from the hospital. He's a little worried about you after last night's incident.'

'What do you mean? Did I scare him off last night? I know I flirt with him sometimes, but I never meant anything too serious by it, I mean I guess I did but I never wanted to make him uncomfortable or upset, I promise.'

'Mr Bartelli, relax, he will explain soon.' Doctor Abrahms sighed, interrupting my thoughts. I could feel the anxiety growing inside me.

After spending the rest of the day walking around the hospital with the nurse, I decided to spend some time strolling the halls on my own. I was a somewhat tired out, but it wasn't a big deal. I enjoyed being able to move around all by myself and it was peaceful having some time alone. Tiring myself out would help me get a better sleep anyway.

When I made it back to the room, Nathaniel was sitting on the chair next to my bed waiting. He looked extremely stressed out and worried.

'Hey, there you are!' He got up from the chair, his eyes were beaming at mine. He tried to help me into bed, but I was fine. He sounded like he was really worried about me.

'I just went for a walk.' Obviously... He seemed a lot calmer after I got myself onto the bed. 'You seem extremely stressed out. Are you Okay?'

I felt his eyes question me, as if something was weird about me asking him for a change. Nathaniel seemed a little puzzled.

'Oh, um, I'm good thank you. Sorry, I just didn't expect that. My brain was just preoccupied, honestly, I've just been really worried about you.'

'About me? Why?'

'Why?' he repeated. 'Because you're going to be out of here soon and I'm worried you are going to be too stubborn to ask for help from anyone. I'm scared you're going to hurt yourself. After yesterday, how do you know this couldn't happen again while you are alone?' There was sympathy in his voice and it just irritated me more.

'Seriously? Are you just pitying me? I think I'll be just fine all by myself. It's just crutches. People have had to deal with much worse. I think I'll be able to manage.' I rebutted; it might have come off slightly harsher than intended. I could see the shock in his face as his eyes widened after taking in what I said.

'What? No, I... I didn't mean it like that. I just... what if something happens to you, who will you call for help?'

'I didn't think that this was what we were going to talk about. I'll be fine, if anything happens, I'll deal with it.' But Nathaniel probed.

'Look, Jacob, I know you might not use it, but I have a number for a company. They can send someone out to help you if you need.'

'Nathaniel, stop it. I'll be fine, it's only temporary and I wouldn't be able to afford anything like that anyway but thank you.' He looked defeated. His eyes were focused on the floor, he was twiddling his thumbs and the energy was gone from inside him. The frustration overtook any process of thought from my mind.

'Maybe that wasn't the number that I was hoping for.' No winking, no ambiguity, I was serious, and I wanted him to know it.

Nathaniel frowned; his eyes drooped momentarily.

'Mr Bartelli, I can't do that.' I hated that he called me that.

'Yeah, I know, I guess I just wanted to try my luck and see.' My heart dropped and now I felt like the one who was defeated. Had I been imagining things? Maybe I was reading too much into everything. It was hard for me to contain myself in this moment. I reached for my crutches, I just needed to get out of the situation.

'No, it's not that' Nathaniel fought on. 'I'm just, I'm still not sure how ready I am to move on, but on top of that, I'm still your nurse and you're still my patient at the end of the day and while that is still the case, it would be inappropriate for me to give you my number.'

I didn't really know what to think, but damn did I feel like an idiot. What was I thinking? Obviously, he wouldn't be able to give me his number. I hadn't even thought of it from a professional aspect. I took the pen and paper from him and I wrote down my number and slid it to him. Then I grabbed my crutches and got up.

'You take my number instead. If you're ready or interested then you let me know. If not, that's perfectly fine. The ball is in your court. I'm going to go for a walk, and I'd appreciate it if I could come back to an empty room. Despite what you think, I'm more than capable of doing this by myself, I'm not some wreck that needs everybody's help.'

I walked out of the room. No other words were spoken from me or Nathaniel and I didn't look back. However, once I made my way out of the room, I leaned against the wall for just a moment and within a few seconds I heard a sound that let me know exactly what the situation was. Nathaniel had torn up the piece of paper.

CHAPTER 4

Discharged

Today was finally the day, after just over two weeks of being in the hospital. I was excited to be able to leave. I had to have the hospital help organise a taxi for me as I was obviously unable to drive, and I also didn't have a car to drive anyway. The taxi was waiting for me downstairs, so I made my way. I got to see Doctor Abrahms earlier that morning and I thanked her for everything.

Now, Nathaniel had made time to escort me downstairs to the taxi. I'd only seen him a few times since me giving him my number, but we were both acting as if nothing had happened. He didn't mention it and so, neither did I.

We went downstairs and Nathaniel opened the door and helped me into the taxi.

'Thank you for these past couple of weeks Nathaniel, I truly appreciate how much you and Doctor Abrahms helped me and I'm sorry… if I was a pain at all.' He blushed while his grin reached both ears, a mysterious look in his eyes.

'You're welcome, more than welcome. Hopefully I get to see you again soon, not that I want you to get injured or anything like that. Take care of yourself and don't rush into things too quickly.' He closed the door and waved me goodbye as I left.

Sleep was not a privilege I was entitled to have last night, so I rested my head on the window of the taxi. It wasn't until we left the hospital that it all hit me. I was in a car, a moving, driving car. At the sudden realisation, I felt my chest tighten, my lungs felt like they were shrinking, and I could hear the short, sharp breaths that were coming from my mouth. My heart was racing, and I could feel my whole body heating up.

The driver looked at me, absolutely distraught. 'Are you all right sir?'

'Yes, I'm just, it's my first time being in a car since the accident and I...' I was talking very fast.

The driver interrupted me by putting my window down. It took me by surprise and shook me out of my panic attack, slightly.

'Take deep breaths, sir. I've picked up many patients from the hospital and it's quite common for people to react after being in an accident. I will drive slowly, and we can take our time. Do you want to talk about something to distract you?'

At first, I didn't want to because I felt awkward and didn't know where to start. Then I just started talking. I told him about the accident and how it had happened, then I told about Judith and her family. I also talked to him about Doctor Abrahms and how she was such a beautiful woman with the most amazing tone in her voice. I told him about how much she cared for me and the amount of effort she put in to try and make me feel good. When I mentioned the topic of Nathaniel and discussed what had happened, the driver gave me a strange look. It seemed to say, 'Oh you're gay,' mixed with 'Please don't do anything'.

The remainder of the drive was slightly more awkward but thankfully it was only a few more minutes before I reached my home. When we finally arrived, I learnt that the hospital had already previously paid the driver when I tried to give him my own money. I felt so grateful. It was yet another gesture that made me feel so much more alone now.

The stairs up to my apartment took a fair amount of energy out of me. It took me a moment to make it to my door. Once I made it inside the apartment, I had a little bit of a hunger ache, but I realised that most of the food would be expired considering the time that I was in hospital. I had to go shopping but I was exhausted, and I had to figure out how I was going to do this. I had no car, not that I'd be able to drive it anyway, on top of that, I had no clue how I would even carry anything. I contemplated asking my neighbour for some help, but I thought twice about that. I decided I'd walk to the supermarket, as it wasn't too far away, and then I could just catch a bus back home.

'Exhausted' is an understatement when describing how I felt after my hike to the shops. I hated that I was so slow doing everything. It was difficult to balance the groceries and I couldn't carry too many bags, but even then, it took me a while to walk. When I got home, I decided that I'd do the rest of the shopping online for the next couple of weeks. For now, I needed to eat. My body was at a tug of war with itself, the rumbling of my stomach was pulling against the drowsiness of my brain. My stomach fell and the drowsiness pulled a little harder…

I woke up to my stomach coming back for another battle, but this time there was no opponent. A simple grilled cheese for breakfast was enough to satisfy my hunger for the moment, or maybe two. Sitting down for breakfast, I thought about what I was going to do for the rest of the day, heck, what I was going to do for the next couple of weeks. I couldn't do any work from home at the moment and when I asked my work if there was anything I could do they had nothing to give me because they were insisting that I had a proper rest. I suppose I could try to look for a new car, but I couldn't exactly test it out or anything like that, and I didn't need it now anyway.

I spent most of the day trying to clean what I could around the house. It turned out that just because you're out of the house, doesn't mean the dust won't accumulate. It wasn't too difficult but there were a few knocks and bumps, evident in my throbbing toes. By the time I had finished, I was sweating, and my arms were aching.

The next step was to have a shower to freshen up. It was awkward and uncomfortable trying to wash myself with the cast while also trying to keep it dry. I almost slipped but I got there in the end and it felt good.

I settled for a microwave meal for dinner because I was in no position to cook and I didn't want to order anything in.

It was quite depressing having dinner by myself in front of the television. It was going to be a lonely couple of weeks. It didn't take long before the tiredness pushed me off the couch and into my bed, I tried browsing on my phone but eventually I dozed off to sleep.

Chirping birds and intruding sunlight interrupted my dreams and brought my soul to waking. It had been a couple of days since I'd left the hospital and I was somewhat proud of being able to care for myself. But naturally, the demons controlling my life decided to divert the tracks of that train…

It started with breakfast. I began to choke on a piece of bread, and it sent me into a coughing fit that made my eyes water as well my throat ache. Lunch was fine, but the shower afterwards was not so great, as I slipped in the shower. The pain wasn't so bad, but there was a high level of frustration that started to brew more and more within me, as I felt so weak and helpless. It took me some time to get back up and out of the shower, drying myself from the water and from more tears. It was time to get my shit organised. I wasn't going to feel sorry for myself all the time.

Getting through the rest of the day seemed like the most tedious and boring task that I had to accomplish. I called one of my friends to see if they wanted to do something, but he was busy for the day. I decided to instead watch some TV until I was ready to make dinner. I was starting to get reckless. For some reason, even though I'd barely done anything all day, I still felt exhausted and drained.

For dinner, I felt like something fresh and more satisfying than a premade frozen meal. So, I prepared a crumbed chicken schnitzel on the stove and fried some chips. Nothing too fancy. But it gave me something to do and it would feel a lot more satisfying. When I plated my food, and tried to sit down, a jolt pinched into my arm, and my reflexes forced my arm to jerk back and I lost my grip. The plate fell to the floor and shattered, and my food was lying on the floor, teasing me.

It took me a minute to register and soak in what just happened. Once I did, I instantly felt my body fuel up with anger and frustration. My eyes were clouding up and my body was shaking. I walked to the couch, grabbed one of my crutches and swung it into my couch repeatedly. I had had enough, and I needed to release the anger that was building up within me. I was screaming, both from frustration and from pain, I kept attacking the couch, in a cathartic rhythm, until I didn't anymore. I was too tired to keep this going so I forced myself to calm down, take some deep breaths and relax.

After giving in, I had to make a microwave meal, yet again, and I sank into the couch for what felt like the most depressing and lonely meal in a long time. I had to remind myself that tomorrow was a new day, that things would get better, I only had a couple of weeks until it was time to go back to the hospital for my check-up. So, I ate my dinner, put on some music, and gave myself some time to ease myself.

Once I finally calmed myself down, I began enjoying my own company for the first time in a while. After about 20 minutes or so, my phone rang with an unknown caller ID. I always hate picking up private numbers, but something told me I needed to pick it up because it could have been Mum, and I did.

'Hello?' I answered, curious as to who was calling me at this time of the night.

'Hello Jacob!' It was Mum, just as I'd thought, she had called to see how everything was going at home and to say that they were in Italy.

I still hadn't told her about what happened, so they were all unaware. They, my mother, father, and younger brother Zach, were enjoying themselves. The flight had been lengthy, but it was easy, and the weather was 'invitingly sunny' to quote my mother. I was happy that they were having a good time, but selfishly I also wanted my mother to help take care of me and I missed my family. I knew it wouldn't be too long before they'd be home. I'd rather save her worries for later. I continued listening to Mum about their trip and everyone said hello and sent their best wishes. I knew there would not be too much of an issue, but I didn't want her to stop everything for me.

I told her I couldn't wait to see all the photos when they got back home. I spoke to Dad who was almost ready to fly back home and Zach who was having the time of his life.

When Zach handed the phone back to Mum, she sounded a little bit more serious.

'Jacob, I wanted to ask you something. I was just wondering if you'd be all right if we stayed for another week?'

'Yeah of course, why would it bother me? Do I need to take care of anything over at your house while you're gone?' I was a little torn at first, but I could never drag them back home just to take care of me. Mum is probably going to be upset when she gets back, and she realises that I didn't tell her about my accident. She still thinks that I'm her baby, but I just want them to enjoy their holiday with no stress from me.

We talked for a little while longer and then we ended our conversation. She asked if I would be able to pick them up from the airport when they got back but I obviously physically couldn't, so I had to make up an excuse about why I wouldn't be able to. I told them that

I'd meet them at the house afterwards instead. I didn't think I was looking forward to that happening, but I supposed it was inevitable.

About a minute after hanging up, the phone rang again. Just when I thought I was going to get some rest. I picked up the phone.

'Mum, what could you have possibly forgotten?' I asked.

'… Is that always how you answer the phone?' said a voice that I couldn't quite put a face to.

'Oh sorry, wait, who is this?' I asked, confused.

'This is Nathaniel, from the hospital…'

'Wait, what? How did you get my number?' I was confused, I thought he…

'From what I recall, you gave it to me. You do remember that right, or was it a mistake?'

'No no, I just thought. I heard you tearing up the paper when I left the room and I just, I assumed you didn't want it.'

'I saved your number before I tore it up, I didn't realise you were waiting, listening in, sorry.' His voice was soft and sympathetic, with a calmness that I most definitely needed today.

'It's fine, I was just confused, and shocked too I guess, but now I'm curious and intrigued.' Thank goodness, he couldn't see my face through the phone because I could already feel it colouring, I felt so stupid, I had been trying, successfully might I add, to ignore what had happened at the hospital. I guess maybe I was right about Nathaniel after all, but I didn't want to jump to any conclusions. If only I could get paid to overthink so much.

So, we got to talking. He asked how I was coping with everything even though it had only been three days. I wasn't going to tell him about today because he would worry, and he would probably get angry at me too. I think he knew or suspected something though because he kept probing me about my day and whether I had been managing everything the last couple of days and how it had been shopping and cooking.

Eventually, I caved in. I took the bait and I told him about what happened during the day and that it was a lot harder than I thought it would be. However, I reassured him that I was Okay, and that I was adapting into the rhythm of everything. Then I told him about my parents staying back a week.

He sounded upset and tried to tell me that I should have been honest with them, but I explained to him why I didn't tell them. He told me it wasn't the smartest decision, but that he understood and respected why I thought they should enjoy their holiday.

I asked about how his week had been, to try and shift the attention away from me and also because I wanted to know.

Thankfully he'd had a good week, but apparently, the hospital wasn't as entertaining without me.

I asked him about Doctor Abrahms, who apparently had encouraged Nathaniel to call me. He was nervous about doing so but obviously managed to do it in the end.

'Doctor Abrahms means a lot to me, she welcomed me very openly when I first started at the hospital. It's been less than four years, but she has trained me, taught me, protected me, and mentored me in ways I could never have imagined. That's why I feel so close with her and she likes to know what's happening in my life, so I tend to tell her pretty much everything. She's like another mother that cares for me in a way that's different and it's reciprocated, I care for her so much and it just feels like she's always been there,' he said.

I could hear him starting to choke up a little bit, his voice was cracking, and I wasn't sure whether to probe and ask more or just leave it. I decided on the latter. I didn't want to push any boundaries.

It was starting to get late and I hadn't realised that we'd been talking for such a long time. I was starting to feel the drowsiness catching up to me.

'Nathaniel, I'm so sorry, but I'm struggling to stay awake…' I felt so guilty, and I didn't want to stop talking to him, but I didn't want to fall asleep on him either.

'Yeah, it's getting late. I hadn't noticed the time. Friday at 7pm, be ready,' he said with confidence in his voice.

'Okay, that's a specific time to call. Could you send your number? It was on private and usually I ignore them.'

'Yes of course! But I meant a date, at 7pm on Friday, I'll pick you up and we will enjoy our night out!' He sounded extremely positive and very relaxed at the same time.

'A date?' I had to make sure I heard correctly.

'Yes, that's Okay with you, right?'

'Y… Yes of course, but you are aware that I'm slightly injured? You did just nurse me out of hospital. Where are we going?'

'That's a surprise and don't worry, it won't be anything too fancy or anything physically demanding.' He said, sounding very smug over the phone. I could just imagine the mandatory smirk and wink that went along with his voice. 'Goodnight Jacob, make sure you get some rest.'

'Goodnight Nathaniel' I said, hiding my nerves and the excitement of what just happened. Shortly after we hung up, he sent his number in a message and just like that, he was all I could think about all night long. It took me some time to get to sleep after I lay in bed. Eventually I closed my eyes, smiling, and let my mind fade into its own thoughts.

CHAPTER 5

Confrontation

Tonight was my date with Nathaniel. I had about eight hours to kill before he picked me up and I could already feel the nerves fluttering around in my stomach. We'd been messaging each other ever since our phone call but he preferred not to text as much for some reason, I guessed it just isn't really his thing. He hadn't budged at all on where we are going so I didn't really have a clue what to wear. I assumed we'd be going to eat somewhere, and he'd said several times that casual will be fine, not the stereotypical gay over-the-top casual, just casual.

Somehow, I had to spend several hours distracting myself from being nervous. But there isn't really much for me to do. I went through my closet to try and figure out my outfit and settled on something that was a mix between casual and comfortable, considering my restrictions. It didn't take long before I found an outfit. I won't bother having a shower right now, I thought, I'll wait until later. I made a sandwich and watched TV.

My parents were getting back next week. Their plane was to arrive in the morning and they thought I was meeting them after work. But I was going to surprise them at the house. I could meet them at the airport although I'd rather avoid going there. It's always hectic at the airport and I was also a little anxious as to how my Mum was going to react so I thought it would be better to deal with it at home. This wasn't exactly the first time I kept a secret from my family. I think she will calm down once she actually realises that everything is fine.

I had a nap and woke up a little later than I'd expected. My heart panicked for the moment until I checked my phone and realised the time. I had about an hour before Nathaniel would be here to pick me up. I had a steaming hot shower that lasted a little longer than it should've, but it felt amazing. I only had about 30 minutes to get ready. I needed to get dry, dressed and fix my hair. I tried on the jeans I'd put aside but they were really tight, and it was hurting my leg after the shower, so I took them off for a moment. I had shorts set aside in case and they were a lot more comfortable. Either option took me way too long to put onto my body. I dried my hair with the towel instead of the blow-dryer because it's always safer to style, then I used some wax to shape it.

About two minutes into fixing my hair, I heard a knock on the door. Could that be him already? There was still 20 minutes to go before he was due. Maybe he was early, but I didn't hear my apartment buzzer ring.

I hopped to the door. I had wax in my hands and only my trunks on. I peeped through the hole but didn't see anyone. I opened the door slowly and Nathaniel sneaked in front of the door. He looked absolutely stunning. It was strange not seeing him in scrubs. I got to see how different he looked outside of work. He looked sexy; his dark, blackish jeans fit him perfectly, shaping all the right places, and he had a light blue top that looked simple and clean. He'd styled his hair back, but it was also angled to the side. His eyes glimmered, meeting mine, he smiled, then he looked down at me and couldn't help but giggle...

'Fuck!' I exclaimed. I was still in my underwear, wax half in my hand and my hair. 'Sorry, I still need to get ready, you're earlier than I thought, and I usually don't take this long, but I've got this whole injury slowing me down. Do you want to come in?'

'Well hello to you too,' he smirked, looking down more than he was looking up. 'I'd love to come in. It usually takes a couple more dates before they start taking off their clothes.' He teased, I let him inside and he planted himself on the couch. 'Take your time, mind if I look around?'

'Not at all, go ahead! There isn't too much to give you a tour of,' I yelled out as I hopped back into the room to get ready. I quickly fixed my hair, pulled on those jeans, and decided on a clean white shirt. I grabbed my crutches and made my way back out. As soon as Nathaniel realised I was coming he stood right up and stared at me. His smile was growing wider on his face.

'Ugh, sorry about before, and sorry for making you wait.' I felt embarrassed, subconsciously scratching my head as a coping mechanism.

'It's fine, I have seen you in a hospital gown before, plus, I did come early. You look amazing by the way.' He was fluttering his eyes up and down my body.

'Thanks, are my cheeks on fire yet? I can feel them burning. You look stunning, extremely stunning. Like, are you sure you still want to do this? By the way, your casual is way sexier than mine.'

'Sexier? I'll keep that in mind.' He winked at me with his glowing, colourful eyes. 'Are you ready to go? Do you need me to help you at all?' His voice was sympathetic.

'No, thank you though, and yes I'm ready.' I smiled, opening the door to let him out and tried to follow behind him but he made me go first.

We made our way down the stairs, which took me a moment, and got to his car. I didn't really know what kind of car it was, but it looked nice and it was cleaner than mine ever was. He walked ahead of me, which wasn't very hard to do, and opened the door for me, helping me get into the passenger seat. 'Thank you, I like the car by the way.'

It was officially my second time getting into a vehicle after my accident. Being the passenger and the fact that I was on a date helped me force myself to internally maintain composure. We were about to take off when he asked if I had any requests. I had no clue what he meant, but when I asked, he clarified: 'any song requests?' Obviously, I had song requests, anything by Rihanna or Beyoncé, but I was interested to see what kind of music he listened to, so I told him 'No, it's Okay, play something that you like.'

The first couple of songs that played, I didn't really know. They were a little different from the songs I listened to, more alternative and soothing. Focusing on the music aided me to forget about being in a car. They were relaxing to listen to, but I think Nathaniel was aware that I didn't exactly know the songs he was playing because the next song he played was one of my favourites. Right from the opening of the song I knew what it was, 'Fool in Love' by Rihanna. 'I love this song.' I was energised by the sound of it.

'Yeah, I know.' Nathaniel smiled after looking at my face.

I contorted my face, raising my eyebrow at him.

'Wait, what do you mean you know? How did you know?' I asked, I was a little intrigued and a tad worried.

'You listened to it a lot in the hospital, sometimes you'd sing it as well, amongst some other songs…' the smug smile on his face was teasing me.

'I was always alone when I was singing!' I turned up the volume, poked my tongue out at him cheekily and started singing.

A few moments later, Nathaniel pulled into a spot and parked the car. I looked around to try and find the restaurant or café, but I'm assuming we're going to have to walk for a little.

'Are we here?' I asked.

'Obviously…' his sarcasm was almost as sassy as mine. I rolled my eyes and laughed.

He got out of the car and told me to wait so he could open the door for me and help me out. I gave him a look and reached to open the door myself, but he locked the door, stalling until he got to the door. He came around, opened the passenger door, and took the crutches from my hand. I felt his hand grasp onto mine and he helped lift me onto my feet. He then handed me my crutches back and helped me.

'If you were able to walk properly, I'd make you close your eyes, but that might be a little hazardous. I could carry you?' he proposed.

I think he wanted to hold my hand while we walked to wherever it was, we were going because he was right up against me. I would have liked to hold his hand too, but unfortunately my hands were occupied. I couldn't stop staring at him, I was so nervous but whenever I looked at him, I felt the nerves ease away. I knew it was still early, but something just felt right.

We kept walking, not for too long, I kept focusing my gaze on Nathaniel. In front of me, there was an uneven brick in the path, and I didn't notice it until I hit the ground…

By the time I registered what had happened, Nathaniel had his face in front of mine checking if I was Okay. I opened my eyes, laying on the ground, and I couldn't help but burst out into laughter. I could just imagine how it would have looked to watch me falling over. Nothing makes me laugh more than seeing people fall over. Then I saw Nathaniel's reaction. His eyebrows made a confused look, a mix of worry and confusion. The look on his face made me laugh even louder. Nathaniel eventually forced out a worried laugh and asked if I was all right, and I was.

Shortly afterwards, we were in front of a restaurant when Nathaniel told me that this was our spot for the night. It was a beautiful Italian restaurant that was exquisitely designed with a modern interior mixed with an Italian style. There were fairy lights set up that helped create a romantic atmosphere. Once inside, we were escorted to our reserved table. I had heard of this place before, but I'd never actually eaten here, I used to go to the beach nearby quite often. It was only down the road from here.

We sat down, ordered our food, and got to talking again. It was quite clear that I was a little nervous. I could feel my heart pumping. When I looked into his eyes, I couldn't tell if he was too.

'Are you nervous? Usually I can tell, this time I can't.' I'm not sure why I asked. I guess I thought it was just better to be real and honest.

He laughed softly; his eyes were focusing on mine.

'I'm always nervous, but I feel comfortable with you.' I had to bite my lip to stop myself from blushing but I'm not too sure if it helped. 'What about you?'

'What about me?'

'Are you nervous? You seem nervous compared to the confident guy that was at the hospital.' He teased.

'Uh, yes I'm a little nervous, I didn't think anything would have come of all that in the hospital, it helped me enjoy my stay. Weirdly enough, the confidence thing is more of a coping mechanism, I guess. It was more of a comforting technique when I was by myself but knowing now that I'm on a date with you, I have to try and impress you.' I did start off kind of strong.

'Well, for what it's worth, the confidence worked on me and I was already impressed before tonight so don't be too nervous.' We exchanged smiles at each other while the waitress brought over some water.

'Anyway, what should we talk about?' I hate when people ask me that.

'That's never a good sign, not knowing what to talk about. Why don't we get to know each other a little more? Tell me a little more about yourself. I always find it interesting, learning about people's lives and stories.'

'Alright, well as you already know, I'm a nurse and while it took me a moment to realise what I wanted to do, I'm now really enjoying my work even though it's only been a couple of years. Before you ask, no, it doesn't bother me that I'm the nurse and not the doctor. I only work part time and I spend a lot of my spare time reading and watching shows, but lately I've been picking up some extra shifts. I used to have a second job, but I let it go not too long ago. I'm trying to get into a full-time schedule at the hospital.'

I could honestly listen to him talk for hours on end. His voice always made me feel warm. It was soothing and mesmerising. He always sounded passionate and his body language just made me feel… oh crap! It's been like two seconds and I think I'm already starting to feel something. I didn't think I should jump right in.

'So, What's your favourite book?' I probed.

'Oh, no no no, before we get into 21 questions, you need to tell me about you! Tell me something about your life.' He made me chuckle.

'Well, my name is Jacob, I'm 24 years old and this is *dun dun* my story. Basically, I work for an auditing company and I'm one of the head auditors in the environmental department. I help to write articles of what we find within the different businesses that we audit, solely focusing on restaurants and food stores. It's similar to the health codes but it's more from a social perspective as well as health codes. I usually work four days a week, but it can vary depending on the schedules. I also enjoy reading, watching television shows and I enjoy playing video games if I have the time. I think you're quite aware of my love for music, specifically Rihanna and Beyoncé.

I'm obviously not working at the moment due to the accident, but I've just been trying to keep myself busy. So, how come you left the second job? That was the place you recommended I call for help, right?'

'Yeah, that was the place.' His eyes were darting around, I could see he was thinking about something. 'It was where my ex-boyfriend worked, it didn't end very well and so I quit him and quit the job.'

'Fair enough, sorry for prying. We can talk about it if you would like.'

'On our first date? No, not really, maybe another time.'

'It's fine, it isn't my business anyway.' I was curious but I knew my place.

Nathaniel started smiling and randomly said 'I don't have one.'

'I'm sorry, what? Don't have one what?' I was so confused; did I miss something?

He laughed a little and then continued, 'A favourite book. There are a few in the top five of my lists. Actually, it's hard to choose even that, I've read a lot of books that I love. What about you, do you have a favourite?'

I had to think about it for a while, as it was hard to pick a favourite. 'Hmm, maybe 'To Kill a Mockingbird' or 'The Kite Runner', I can't really pinpoint it to just one.'

'Both are extremely amazing novels. Have you got any other favourites? Movies, singers, TV shows?'

'I think my favourite movie is 'The Lovely Bones', and Rihanna and Beyoncé as previously mentioned and 'Grey's Anatomy'.' He laughed and teased me for about five minutes but then admitted that he also used to watch Grey's Anatomy, as it's an amazing show after all.

I learnt that his favourite movie was 'The Lord of the Rings' trilogy. He was surprised and confused when I told him I hadn't watched any of them. It's safe to say at least half the restaurant turned and stared at us when he yelled 'What!?' I couldn't stop laughing. He didn't have a favourite singer or a song, which made sense considering he listens to a variety of different songs. His favourite show was 'Game of Thrones', which I've only seen a few episodes of. It was interesting to learn more about him and what he enjoys in life.

While we were talking, the waiter started bringing out our meals. We both ordered a pasta and a woodfired pepperoni pizza to share, sided with a glass of wine. I've never really enjoyed wine, but I wasn't going to be rude. We learnt more about each other throughout the dinner; Nathaniel, for some strange reason, loved winter while I preferred summer, we both enjoyed dogs over cats, but he still has a love for them and I love chocolate ice-cream although he prefers vanilla and lemon. Vanilla though… really?

The pasta tasted extremely delicious and almost filled me up entirely, but the pizza melted in my mouth and satisfied my stomach as the cherry on top. We talked for a while throughout the dinner and then we eventually got the bill, skipping dessert because we were both full. The pizza was as delicious as the pasta, if not more.

When I reached for the bill, he smacked my hand and gave me a stern look that said something along the lines of, 'don't even think about it!' That didn't stop me, I gave him a look back and reached for the bill again, but he smacked my hand away once more.

'Don't' he said firmly, holding his gaze.

'I'm more than happy to pay, or even split, at least let me pay for half.' I pleaded.

'Not a chance gorgeous.' He made me blush and smile, but anyone listening would have gagged, myself included.

He paid for the dinner, hopped up around and helped me get out of my seat. Then, we made our way outside and he held the door of the restaurant for me so I could easily make my way outside. And they say chivalry is dead, whomever 'they' is. I assume my injury was also encouraging him to be like that but I wasn't complaining. Maybe once I recovered, I'd be able to repay the kindness and take him out on a date.

We exited through the same door that we entered, and I turned to walk back to the car but before I could get anywhere Nathaniel grabbed my arm to move me around. I shot him a questioning look.

His response was: 'We're not done just yet.' He winked as he helped spin me around.

'Oh, where are we heading?'

'Always so inquisitive, aren't you? We are just going for a walk, possibly ending up at a particular place that for now will remain a surprise. Plus, if you know this place the way you mentioned, you'll know exactly where we are going.'

I smiled at him and he returned the gesture. I knew exactly where we were going, but I wasn't sure if he was the biggest fan. The beach. We stopped by at the ice-cream store on the way there. It was extremely awkward for me to walk with my crutches while holding the ice-cream, so I slowed down a tad.

'Do you want me to hold it for you?'

'No, thank you, but I'll manage.' I smiled at him; I was almost finished anyway.

'You're welcome, just don't stress your hands too much, you might get another of those cramps.' He winked. I choked on my ice-cream from laughter which made me twitch into a coughing fit, my eyes watering up, which led to a lack of control over my ice-cream. It splatted on the floor before I knew what was happening.

'Shoot, I'm so sorry,' he said giggling and still teasing me. 'We can go back if you'd like!'

'No no, it's fine, you just caught me off guard. Now I'm a mess.' My face was all red and my shoes had ice-cream on them. I was sweating from the laughter and my teary eyes felt heavy, interfering with my vision.

'Still looking good to me. It's fine, I'm sorry, I didn't think you'd choke and drop the ice-cream.' He gave me a slight nudge with his elbow and smiled at me apologetically.

'Ahh fuck! My ribs!' I yelled.

'Oh shit, I forgot, I'm sorry!'

I couldn't hold in my laughter. 'My ribs are fine, I'm just messing with you.' I winked at him teasingly.

The glare that I received was a very intense mix of embarrassment, anger and sarcasm.

'You actually had me worried you know! I'm going to smack you! Okay not smack you, but don't pull that on me! I felt so bad!' His voice was shaky and worried. I think I threw him off guard more than I intended to. His face dropped a little, so I had to cheer him up. I gave him a smile and quickly sneaked a bite of his ice-cream.

'Hey!' he shrieked in reaction.

'I would eat mine but it's on the floor and now yours looks way better. Plus, it's still edible,' I pleaded.

'That's it, we're going back to get you another ice-cream.' He started walking back. I told him I was just teasing but he ignored my plea. 'Wait here.' He commanded and then started off into a jog.

'Hey, no fair, I'm injured! Let me come with…' He was too far away now; the shop wasn't too far a distance though. Resting on the side of the pathway I only waited a couple of minutes and then I saw that Nathaniel was making his way back. He had bought himself a second cone and had another one his hand for me. Stubborn man, but I was still grateful either way. He was smiling like a fool, and honestly, so was I.

When he reached me, he handed me one of the cones and we kept walking as if nothing had happened.

'Thank you.' I said, smiling at him. I was still surprised that he'd actually gone back.

We made our way to the beach and it felt so good just to even see the sand. I could feel the smile on my face grow immediately. The beach always made me blissful. I turned to face Nathaniel.

'Can we sit on the sand?'

He answered with a nod, leading the way down the beach until we found a spot to sit. When we did, it took a moment for me to sit. I reached down for my shoes and instinctively lifted my leg and winced.

'What's wrong?' he asked anxiously.

'Nothing, I'm just taking my shoes off to feel the sand.' I calmed him. It was a struggle to get them off, but I could reach if I stretched. Nathaniel wanted to take them off for me, but I scolded him, then apologised and politely declined his offer. That would be too demeaning for me and I wanted to do it myself. Although it took me some time and a lot of effort, I eventually managed to get my shoes off. Sliding my toes into the cold sand was an amazing feeling, it was relaxing and soothing on my skin. I could never not love this feeling.

'How about I take off your shoes?' I joked to him, turning the tables.

'Are you into that? Are you telling me about your foot fetish?' He teased and laughed.

'No!' I chuckled lightly, 'Don't you want to feel the sand?'

Nathaniel smiled at me 'I'm feeling the sand with my hands, that's satisfying enough for me. I'm just glad that you're enjoying yourself.'

I thought about the night I was having and where we'd ended up.

'I am. Wait, is something wrong? Are you not having a good time?' Was I that boring? I hate that it felt like he was nursing me again.

'No, nothing is wrong at all. I think the night has gone well so far!' It didn't sound like he was lying or anything like that, but it just felt like something was off.

'May I ask, do you not like the beach?'

He sounded slightly defeated. 'It's not exactly my favourite place.'

'Oh, then why are we here?' I wasn't sure if it came across in my speech, but I was extremely confused, and I felt like this wasn't going the best way.

'Well you mentioned tonight at dinner that you enjoyed the beach a lot and it was close, so I just thought why not, plus I enjoy the walk. I wanted to try and make you happy.' He admitted, smiling at me. That made my eyes tear up a little. He was listening, and he just wanted to impress me, which I was extremely flattered by.

'Sorry that I'm not the best at walking, but why don't we compromise? Let's walk on the beach.' I insisted, raising my eyebrow at him.

'Are you sure that you are up for it? It's going to be more tiring for you than it is for me.'

'Yes, of course I'm sure. Worst case scenario I end up with another cramp.' I winked after that last comment. He helped me get up and we started heading back towards the car, but we continued along the shore. He seemed a little distant so I teased him.

'This would be cuter if you could hold my hand huh?'

'I suppose so' he responded dryly, sounding disappointed.

He was walking ahead of me, a little aimlessly but he still seemed to be somewhere else. I was close enough to nudge him with one of my crutches, so I did, lightly. He turned around and raised an eyebrow at me. He looked like a confused puppy with that face, I could just cuddle him, or tackle him... I dropped my crutches, he started walking towards me to pick them up and then, when he was close enough, I took the opportunity and pounced on him, tackling him down to the sand and ruffling his hair. He looked me dead in the eye with his gracious gaze.

'What the hell was that for?' he said.

I held his gaze and felt a pain in my leg which made me cringe, then I started laughing with his body held beneath mine, pinning him down in my arms. My laughter, like a flu, spread contagiously to Nathaniel, a chuckling sound released from his lips and growing into a confused but uncontained laughter. I could tell he thought I was crazy. We eased back into our normal selves and watched each other, losing myself deeply in his eyes, I realised I couldn't move, but that didn't take anything away from this moment.

He broke the silence. 'Would you mind if I kiss…' and before he couldn't finish asking, I made my move, planting my lips onto his.

His lips were amazing, soft, and they fit perfectly against mine, my hands gliding against the edges of his face. It lasted a moment before I pulled back and caught my breath and apologised for my abruptness. Within an instant, I felt his hand grab the back of my head and he pulled me back in, placing his lips exactly where they were supposed to be. There was the passionate addition of his tongue that found its way through my lips.

We kept going for a while, we were getting warm and there was the sand in too many places, but it felt wonderful. Once our lips parted I spoke.

'That was amazing. Just so you know, I'm stuck, I can only roll over at this point.' I eventually managed to roll onto the sand and off Nathaniel. 'Also, I think you're getting a cramp!'

He laughed and then nudged at me as I lay on my back against the sand, my head in the crook of his shoulder.

We stayed there peacefully for a while. The sound of the waves soothing our minds, the sand comforting our bodies and the sight of the stars easing our souls. We talked softly about the sky and the world and how he wanted to travel to Europe, to visit a bunch of different countries. I didn't want to leave but a chilling breeze came through, forcing me to shiver.

'Maybe we should head back, it's starting to get a little cold.' He turned to me after he spoke and continued, 'Are you shaking?'

'Just a little, I wish we could just freeze this moment, you know?'

He laughed at me and teased, 'very dramatic and melancholy, we could instead make more moments like this, I'm down if you are.'

He was watching me and was waiting for my response. I didn't even have to think about it.

'Of course, I'm down.' I grinned at him and he responded with a smile and blew me a kiss. Nathaniel helped me up yet again and we walked slowly back towards the car with moonlight reflecting its light over us.

We got to the car, Nathaniel opened the door for me again, and he drove me home. The awkwardness was almost beginning as he parked the car but before it could, Nathaniel hopped out of his seat and helped me out.

'Thank you, for helping me out and for the whole night. I had an amazing time.' I could see him blushing at what I'd said.

'You're welcome. Thank you for giving me a great time.' He leaned in after closing the car door behind me and gave me kiss. This time I could feel his hands grabbing at the back of my head and brushing my hair. It was a nice, breathtaking, and smooth kiss. When we separated, I asked if he wanted to come upstairs. His face contorted as if he was holding something back.

'Um, I'm sorry but, I don't really do the dirty on the first date.'

I spat out laughter. 'Do the dirty? You mean sex? Firstly, who even says that? Second, that wasn't what I meant at all. In fact, I'm actually still…' The confusion in his eyes bore into me, he was waiting for me to finish.

'Still what?'

I looked down at the ground while I continued, 'Still a virgin.' I wasn't too sure how he would take it.

When I raised my head, I saw his eyes widen with surprise.

'Wait, really? I thought… but at the hospital you were so out there and flirtatious.'

'Really. Anyway, I guess I should head upstairs, I've got to deal with my parents tomorrow. Thank you again for tonight.'

As I turned to head back, I heard him yell 'Wait!' He placed his hands on my face, then his lips on mine once more, continuing to kiss me into the night.

Reaching for air he said his final piece. 'It doesn't bother me, that you're still a virgin or whatever, we can go as slowly or as quickly as you please.' That made me smile. It wasn't such a big deal for me. I wasn't exactly holding out just waiting for the right guy. We said our goodbyes and goodnights and we parted ways. I couldn't sleep right away, laying on the bed, I just kept replaying the night over and over in my head, grinning like a fool. Then my heart shuddered as I thought about my parents tomorrow, it was no wonder I was struggling to sleep.

CHAPTER 6

Roots

It was bright and early when the sun started creeping in, a little too early for my liking. It wasn't a comfortable sleep and I wasn't able to doze back off into the calming unconsciousness that I wanted so desperately to reach. I slowly rolled over, making slight manoeuvres even though I didn't want to. Forcing my eyes to open, the phone blinding as it flashed the time. It was only 7:52, why on earth was I awake? I didn't have work and it was a Saturday. Slowly but surely, I crawled out of bed, reached for my crutches and went to the bathroom, then to the kitchen to make breakfast.

I caught the train to my parents' house to meet them there. They were still unaware of the accident. As far as my family knew, I was at work and would be seeing them tonight for dinner. Instead, I got to their house at around lunch, knowing they'd get home in a few hours. I bought some meat so I could prepare food for when they arrived, with the hopes that it would soften the blow.

Time had passed. The late lunch was ready, the salads prepared, the steaks cooked, and the vegetables steamed. I have to say I was a lot more comfortable and capable of cooking. I planned it so that everything would be perfect when they got home, but they still hadn't arrived by 3pm. Maybe their flight was delayed or maybe they were stuck in traffic, visiting someone, or eating on the way home...

I decided to call Mum to learn their whereabouts. I knew they'd be in a taxi, so I wouldn't be distracting them from driving. But what if it distracted the driver of the taxi? I started to hesitate; I wasn't sure what to do. My thoughts were blowing up all around me. I forced myself to press the call button and I instantly calmed down when Mum answered. They were just on their way home, would be here in about ten minutes or so. I told them I was here and thankfully she didn't ask why I wasn't at work. She would see me soon and would then learn about the situation. I mean it wasn't a big deal, but we'd see what happens.

The keys rattled as Mum opened the front door. She walked in first, followed by my brother and father, their suitcases dumped near the door. Soon enough, the smell of the food brought them to the dining area. I was sitting at the table when they walked in. When Mum saw me, she had a look that I will never forget. Happiness, shock, and anger all in one. She screamed, hugged me, kissed me, then slapped me and finally sat down with Dad and Zach, ready to eat and learn what had happened. I told them everything, from the accident, to the hospital, about the other family and even that I went on a date yesterday with Nathaniel.

A deafening sound roared when an open palm connected with my arm. My mum slapped me on the arm.

'Why on earth didn't you tell us?!' she yelled.

'Mum... I already told you that I like guys.'

Another smack followed when I finished my response, a little lighter than the first.

'Not that you idiot! Why didn't you tell us about the accident when we spoke on the phone?!'

'I didn't want to worry you; I didn't want you to stress about me while you were on holiday and I didn't want you to cut your trip short because of me. I was fine, everything worked out and now I'm recovering. I just need one favour, but once you guys have settled and rested. I need to buy a new car, hopefully next week but I need to trust your judgement because, well I obviously won't be able to test it out myself.'

'Of course,' my dad interrupted with excitement, proud of the car knowledge that he has stored throughout his life.

After everything calmed back down, we began to eat, the food was a little cooler than I'd hoped, but nobody complained. I think we were all too hungry to care, I know I was. They told me stories about their holiday and the amount of food that they had eaten. Zach was more than happy with his first overseas trip; he was tanned and full of smiles. I think he was also happy to be home. I was happy that they were home too. I missed them. I barely get to see them as is.

I finally got home, catching the train back because I refused to let my family drive me back as I knew that they would be extremely tired. I also realised that I didn't have plans for the week to come.

Next morning, I made my way back to my parents' house after my father called me telling me he was ready to search for a new car. He clearly wasted no time when it came to cars, and he said he wasn't jet lagged. He was a full-time mechanic for a large portion of his life, and now he worked for a restaurant. But he dealt with cars whenever an opportunity allowed him to. I think he'll probably be back working with cars again one day, but the strain on his body was too much after he had his heart attack. He's only been at the restaurant for a couple of years now and he enjoys it, but cars have always been a big passion for him.

When I got to the house, Dad was already dressed and ready to leave the house. He'd found a few cars online the night before and wanted to show them to me. I personally wasn't too fussy about cars, mainly because I didn't know too much about them, but if they looked nice, worked, and played my music I was happy.

We spent most of the afternoon driving between locations. I couldn't test drive any of them yet because of my leg so I went off what Dad liked to drive. After discussing them, we both settled on the third car that we visited, so we bought it, just like that. The insurance money I received was more than enough, and my Dad managed to do his whole bargaining thing. It was a grey Hyundai of some sort that was a seven-year-old model, but it had the ability to let me connect my music.

I couldn't take the car home straight away, so Mum drove back again with Dad and eventually they both drove back to my apartment, dropping off me and then the car. Mum then invited me over for dinner, and after the day we had the least I could do was spend dinner with them.

They seemed more tired today. I think the jet lag was starting to affect them a little more. There weren't as many questions or stories as there were last night. They tried, well Mum tried, to probe me about my date with Nathaniel, but I didn't spill any details. It's still a little weird discussing my love life with my parents. They don't really need to know about all that yet. They completely accept me and my lifestyle, however I somehow still feel like I'm oversharing whenever I talked about a boy.

I had my last slice of pizza; Mum had been too tired to cook. I got up to make my way home, but they didn't want me to catch the train again. At the same time, I didn't want them to drive me home because they were both clearly too tired and I didn't want to bother them anymore than I already had.

So, we came to a compromise. I'd stay the night at my parents' house, my room here was still the same and I guess there was no harm in spending more time with my family. Mum and Dad were both tired and fell asleep after an hour or so, but Zach was still awake. He seemed excited to be able to spend some time with me. He used to look up to me in a way when we were younger, and I think he still did a little. He was really happy for me when I came out. He took it a lot better than I thought he would have. He's 18 now but he seems a lot older, and I think that was partially my fault.

He asked me about the accident and if I had been scared. I told him the truth.

'I didn't have time to be scared because it all happened so quickly. I couldn't really focus on anything. But at the hospital, when I woke up, I was scared and worried. I wasn't sure which parts of me were injured and which parts weren't.'

'I'm glad you're Okay. I got a little worried yesterday when we walked in. I didn't expect anything like that.' Zach confessed while his phone buzzed off.

'I'm sorry man, I didn't mean to give everyone a scare, but you know Mum, if I had told her over the phone, we both know she would have caught the first flight back just to cook me dinner. I didn't want to be the reason to cut your holiday two weeks short.'

He laughed, lightening up a little, then his phone buzzed again.

'Who keeps messaging you, huh?' I teased, nudging him in the ribs with my elbow.

He blushed a little. 'Just a friend.' I noticed his smile widen as he said it.

'Oh yeah? A guy or a girl?'

'A girl. Only one of us is gay.' He smirked, nudging me back.

'Ahh, so it's not 'just a friend' then,' I winked. 'Is it serious?'

'Umm, not exactly, just trying to see how it plays out, it's hard to figure things out.'

'I feel you man, if you ever want to talk about these things, let me know Zach. I'm always here if you need anything, you know, that right?'

He put his phone away and focused a little more on me.

'I know and I will.' He smiled weirdly; we didn't have these talks as much as we used to.

'And what about your studies, is everything Okay there?' I asked.

'Yeah I'm in my second year now and I'm enjoying it,' he said truthfully.

'I'm glad because engineering is one thing I can't really help you with and I know you're in second year, I'm your brother not some random uncle. What about everything else? Your friends? Mum and Dad?'

'Yeah, everything is fine, I promise.' He sounded a little irritated.

'Sorry with the 21 questions, just want to make sure that everything is Okay. Do you want me to leave you to talk to your friend?'

'No, not at all. I barely even get to hang out with you anymore, I wish we could spend more time together sometimes.'

'I know, I'm sorry about that, we really should hang out more.'

'It isn't only you, we've both busy lately.'

'Yeah I guess so. What about tomorrow? I can stay if you aren't doing anything.'

'That would be awesome! Actually, can I ask for a favour? I, umm, I have a date with my friend tomorrow, and I was wondering if maybe we could go to the shops for some new clothes? We could maybe watch a movie as well.'

'Wow, a date? What time? How did Mum take it? And yes, of course, that sounds like fun.'

'It's a dinner at 7pm and Mum doesn't know that I'm going on a date…'

'Good choice! I'm going to head to sleep and we can think of something to tell her tomorrow. Think of a movie for tomorrow as well! Goodnight little Zach!'

'Goodnight!' he replied gratefully with a smile on his face.

I woke up in a weird déjà vu state, being in my teenage bedroom with my posters still hung up. It was strange to wake up back here. It almost felt like I was 16 years old again, hiding myself in my room. The family were eating at the table when I came down, even Zach was awake, and it was only 8:30. Apparently their bodies still hadn't adjusted.

According to Mum it was my sleeping pattern that was abnormal. Zach informed Mum of our plan for the day, adding that we might be out a little late for dinner. Very smooth of him. Mum and Dad seemed happy to know that we were going to be spending time together, and honestly so was I. You don't realise how much time goes by when you move out until you go back to visit.

We left the house a couple of hours after breakfast and got in Zach's car; I think he heard my deep breaths as he started the car because he turned his face to me. He gave me a questioning and worried look. I told him that it's just a bit of anxiety that happens when I get in a car, that ever since the accident it had been mildly intrusive. Strangely enough, Dad didn't notice anything when he drove me, or if he did, he never mentioned anything about it. I think I freaked Zach out a tad.

'Do you want me to drive slowly or anything like that?' he asked sincerely.

'No, it's fine, I'll get over it eventually. Once we start driving it will go away.'

'Are you taking anything for the pain, or for the anxiety?' Zach asked seriously.

My brother had had a strange time when he was younger. He used to be really depressed. I don't know entirely what it was. I don't think it was one specific thing either, but he was for a couple of years in high school. I don't want to downplay it because in all honesty I'm not exactly sure what happened, Zach never wanted to talk about it and, so we didn't. Anyway, he was on antidepressants for a while and he got highly dependent on them. Trying to focus without them was exceedingly difficult for him, even after he was getting through the depression, he was still attached to the pills. He's fine now. His mental health had been better over the last few years. But it had given Mum and Dad a scare and I was worried he might have ended up doing something too serious for them to handle. Ever since then, he'd always been sceptical about drugs, even prescribed.

'I was taking medicine in the hospital at first, then painkillers at home, for the pain obviously, but I'm not taking anything for it anymore. As for the anxiety, I never really thought about taking anything for and I don't think I will. It's just something that formed after the accident. I know it will smooth out over time.'

'That's good to hear. I'm glad everything is Okay. It's scary to think what could have happened to you.' Zach sounded thankful.

We got to the shopping centre and we decided it would be better to watch a movie first, that way we wouldn't have to carry bags of shopping with us, so we did. We watched a movie called 'The Shallows', it was a thriller shark movie with Blake Lively. It was super intense and scary, not to mention that Blake looked absolutely stunning!

We started shopping after the movie. Zach wanted me to help him pick out an outfit for his date. It was extremely easy to see how nervous he was. I could tell he really liked this girl. We had roughly two hours to shop before he'd drop me off and pick up his date. I told him to sneak in a shower at mine instead of at home, so Mum didn't question anything.

After going through a variety of choices, more as a way to kill the time than annoy Zach, which made him even more nervous, we decided to stay away from a casual look. My brother also didn't like flashy colours, sort of similar to me, so we went for a simpler and more sophisticated look. White shoes, slim black jeans with a nice smooth, light cream button up shirt. I must admit, he scrubbed up well.

'Aren't you glad you have me? You even found some *good* jeans.'

It took him a second, but he realised what I said.

'Shut up!' he retorted. 'We still have heaps of time, what do you want to do?' he asked.

'Well we can spend some time at mine if you'd like, or we can get some books… I wouldn't mind browsing in a bookstore.' I mentioned it more as a request than a suggestion.

We went past the bookstore and it was still open, so we went inside. It didn't take long before I got lost searching the shelves. There were so many books that I wanted but I forced myself to limit it to only three books because there were still several books at home that were untouched. I hadn't realised how long we had been in the store until Zach came and nudged me, telling me that we should probably get going. I paid for the books, we got to the car and Zach drove to my apartment. I tried to keep myself calm while he was driving so that I didn't frighten him or make him worry. When we got to the apartment, he tried to help me up, but I managed to get up the stairs on my own.

We settled in, he had a shower and I cut the tags off the clothes for him. When Zach finally got out of the shower, it was game time. It was pretty obvious that he was getting more nervous as he was getting dressed, but when he stepped out, it was clear that my outfit choice for Zach was perfect. He looked almost complete; his hair needed a bit of touching up. I pushed him into the bathroom and made him face the mirror. I used a bit of hair wax and I styled his hair up. Then, I handed him some deodorant and some cologne, and he was good to go. I asked him if he wanted to quickly use a facial scrub, but he politely denied the offer.

'Good luck Zach. Let me know how it all goes down. I want full details. Remember to have fun and try to relax. If you feel yourself getting too nervous, just take a few deep breaths and if you need an excuse to leave just text me.'

I could see from his demeanour that he was starting to feel excited about the date, even though the nerves were still present.

'Thanks Jacob, for everything today! Hopefully everything goes well, I'll talk to you soon.'

'You're more than welcome. Drive safe!' I said as he walked out of the door. I felt like a proud parent.

CHAPTER 7

The Rundown

A week had passed since Zach's date with his lady friend and I still hadn't talked to him about it. I wanted to give him space and not give Mum anything to be suspicious about. However, enough time had passed, and I was interested to know what how the night went, so I called him.

Zach went over the details, saying that they had laughed a lot and enjoyed themselves. Throughout Zach's recollection of the date I could tell he truly had a wonderful night. Zach continued to tell me about his date and how they talked for hours on end before they actually left the restaurant. When they finally left, he paid for the night, drove her home and then he went for it. He made a move, kissing her, and she kissed back. That apparently continued for a moment before they finally said goodnight to each other.

'What about you?' Zach asked, when he finished recounting the date. 'Didn't you have a date during the week?'

'As a matter of fact, yes, I did, we went on another date a few days ago. Are you… sure you want to hear about my date?' I wanted to make sure that he knew he was asking about a date between two guys.

'Well yeah, why not?' he asked blatantly.

'Alright, well…' I told him about how Nathaniel had organised to pick me up for a lunch. It was another casual surprise. Zach asked if everything had been comfortable in the car and honestly, I didn't remember having any issues when he picked me up.

After we drove, we got to a park and Nathaniel had set up for us to have a picnic. After getting the blanket out and the basket, we sat down in a nice spot under the sun, talked, and ate. It was a really cute and romantic idea and it was something that Nathaniel enjoyed, picnics and parks. I enjoyed myself as well, and since the first date ended up on the beach, he decided to do something more geared towards his tastes. I told Zach I'd spare him the details but basically, we enjoyed ourselves and made out for a while. It all up was a beautiful and lovely date, and thankfully the weather had been on our side.

After concluding my call with Zach, I decided to call work to see if there was anything I could do from home, or even if I could potentially come in and some light duty work. They refused, saying they wouldn't let me do anything without the doctor's approval and that my rest and recovery was more important than rushing straight back into work. I had to get my check up next week, I was going to just go to a local doctor, but Nathaniel had insisted that I go back to the hospital for it.

That afternoon, not too long after lunch, I got a strange phone call from Nathaniel, it sounded as though he had been crying.

'Hello?' I answered.

'Hey, I'm sorry, but can I come by? I just, I don't know who else to talk to.' He sounded panicked.

'Yeah of course, what happened? Is everything Okay?'

'Umm, I'll explain when I get there,' he said before hanging up. It all sounded oddly cryptic and it had me worried.

It only took about 20 minutes before I heard a strong knock on the door. When I opened the door, Nathaniel was standing there, and you could see in his eyes that he had been crying. His body seemed agitated from panic.

'Can I come in please?' he asked nervously.

'Yes, of course, come in.' I moved aside and let him in. He came and sat down on the couch almost instantly. I sat down next to him and put my arm around him to comfort him.

'Do you want a drink or anything? What's wrong? I can tell that you're upset, talk to me.' I got up to get some water and then I stood in front of him.

'Thank you.' He took a sip of the water. 'It's nothing too serious or anything, but could you please sit down again?'

So, I sat down, and it took him a moment to calm down and speak. Dr Abrahms was out of town this week, he said, and wouldn't be back for a couple of days and I think he just wanted someone to talk to. His hands kept fidgeting so out of instinct I grabbed them, held them, and looked at him. I took deep breaths and had him mimic my breathing. His voice sounded shaky when he started talking.

'Just before, this morning, I was out for a walk just getting a coffee and breakfast and I saw him. My ex-boyfriend. Well he saw me and then he came over to say hello. He said he wanted to talk, and I had some free time since I was off work, so we had breakfast together. Everything started to rush back. He was so manipulative when we were together, and he used to play with my mind. One day I discovered that my mind wasn't the only thing that he was playing with. Then I ended it because I had no intention of dealing with a cheat. When we sat to talk at breakfast, he apologised for everything and repeatedly told me how stupid he was, how sorry he was and that he's changed. He was telling me that he missed me, and it was like he was playing with my head all over again. I got upset because I did feel love for him, but he ruined that. I thought that allowing him to have that closure might make things easier for him.'

I felt puzzled. I hadn't really been in Nathaniel's position before and I didn't know what to say. I was also starting to feel a little jealous. Usually I'd help sort the situation out, but this time I didn't want to. I wanted to be the solution.

'We talked a little more and he kept telling me about how he'd felt lost and he'd cheated because he didn't know how to communicate his problems. That didn't make it right, but our relationship was never perfect, and I wasn't exactly easy to deal with either. I was clingy and needy, and I was working a lot too. Anyway, once I was done listening to him, I told him that I didn't want to get back together, I told him that I had moved on and that I was happier without him.

When I got up to leave, he came over and he kissed me... he kissed me and then I kissed him back. Then I pulled away and I said that we were done. He grabbed me with his arm and tried to pull me back. When I backed off, he started to get aggressive with me. He was angry, telling me he still wanted me and that I clearly wanted him. Then he tried to kiss me again and I said no, pulling my face away. He tightened his grip at that point. I did whatever I could to break myself free and then I ran back home. I had no idea what to do and then I called you.'

His red, tear-stained eyes looked into mine as he finished talking. I could feel his blood pulsing through his hands. They were sweating and more tears started rolling down his face. I looked up and wiped them away before leaning in to give him a hug. I held him for a moment, then he hugged me back. He laid his head on my shoulder and rested it there momentarily. After backing away, I got him a glass of water and came back to sit next to him.

'Do you want to do something about your ex?'

'What do you mean?' he asked, confused.

'I mean, do we need to do anything about it, like report it or anything… or take matters into our own hands.' I asked.

'No, I think it will blow over and he'll go away, it just scared me. I'm so sorry by the way,' he said apologetically.

'What are you sorry for? You didn't do anything wrong.' I knew exactly what he was sorry for, but he didn't need to be.

'I'm sorry that I dumped all this on you, I'm sorry that it was all so random and I'm sorry that I kissed him.' He started to get caught up and flustered. 'It just feels like I cheated on you, it makes me feel like him!'

'You don't need to apologise. You've done so much for me; this is nothing in comparison. Regarding your ex, I won't lie, I got a little jealous and all, but I get it, it was just a kiss, and technically we've never had 'the talk'. So, I guess you don't exactly have anything to feel bad about.'

'I guess you're right. Could we do that?' he asked.

'Do what?' I responded.

He looked down and said, 'Can we have 'the talk', so we can like determine everything?' He made it seem like something bad was about to happen.

'Okay, well I guess I'll swallow my pride and I'll go first.' I was noticeably quiet for a moment; Nathaniel was waiting for me to talk and so was I. 'I'll be completely honest here; I really enjoy spending time with you. I really like you and I'd really like it if we continued seeing each other, but at the same time, I totally respect your decision if you want to try and work things out with your ex.'

He looked up at me and had a grin on his face, from ear to ear.

'You're an idiot if you legitimately think that I want to get things sorted out with my ex. To tell you the truth, I enjoy spending time with you also. I know it's only been a few weeks but if you're keen for this, to be exclusive and see where it goes, then I am too.'

His smile grew wider and so did mine. He grabbed me by my shirt and pulled me in for a kiss. Our lips synchronised perfectly, our hands caressing each other as our mouths continued to intertwine.

'So, does this mean that you're my... boyfriend?' I asked, just trying to let the moment sink in, surprised by the conversation that had just taken place. It all felt very sudden, I only just met him not so long ago.

'Yes, I suppose it does. Are you happy with that? I know that we haven't known each other for very long and we haven't spent too much time together, so we don't have to put a label on it if you don't want to' He sounded worried when he asked.

'No, I'm fucking thrilled! Now I don't have to worry about finding a hot boyfriend anymore since I've already got one.' I winked at him; I may have been teasing but I was also dead serious. 'Boyfriend' I repeated, enjoying the way it sounded. Then, I moved back into him and kissed him again before I let him cuddle me while we laid down into each on the couch.

'I must say as weird as it sounds, I'm glad you ran into your ex-boyfriend because it led to you coming over here and now, I have a really hot boyfriend and it feels pretty amazing. I know it might be too soon, but I'm glad we talked about everything and I'm glad we're doing this.'

'Me too' he replied, rubbing my shoulder with his hand while he kissed me on the cheek. I was excited to see where this would take us.

A couple of moments after peacefully laying with each other on the couch, Nathaniel broke the silence with his enlightening voice.

'So, it's only like 1:30. Did you have any plans for the day before I randomly interrupted it?'

I smiled at him, 'I don't think I could have asked for a better interruption. Also, no I didn't have any plans for the day. I'm not sure if you've noticed but I'm still somewhat injured and can't really do much. What were your plans for the day?' I probed.

'I just had a couple of errands to do, but most of them are done anyway, nothing too urgent. Maybe we should go out somewhere, enjoy the day. What do you think?' He seemed extremely eager.

'Are you sure you'd be up for it?' I asked, just to be certain.

'Yes, of course!' He was certain.

'You sound really intrigued, what would you like to do?'

It took some back and forth suggestions before we concluded that we were going to spend some time on a walk, only short due to my leg, then we'd come back and relax together, watching a movie and head to dinner after.

It was nice and sunny outside, but some threatening clouds looked as though they were approaching soon. I was obviously not as fast as Nathaniel, but we walked at a steady, comfortable pace. We had no destination in mind, we just strolled around whilst I told him about some of my favourite places around my apartment: the cafés, supermarket, the barber shop. I didn't live in the city, but in a suburban area close by.

We came across the park and the swings made Nathaniel very excited for some reason, so I pushed him on the swings like a little kid. It was awkward to push him while holding onto my crutches, but I managed to do so. After a couple of minutes, the clouds started closing in, so we started to walk back to my place. Within a few moments it had started to sprinkle. We were about five minutes away from home, at my pace anyway. Then, before we knew it, it started to pour down and we were caught in the middle of it. I gave him a look as if to say I was sorry.

'I'll be able to catch up, you go ahead.' I told him.

'Don't be stupid, hold on to your crutches!' he delegated.

He came over, and picked me up in his arms, as if carrying a baby. My eyes widened with surprise as he effortlessly lifted me up. I did not notice his strength before today. I felt his grip tighten on me and he started running to the house. I couldn't stop laughing. It was hilarious, and he was completely serious too.

'It's just rain,' I said, teasing. He gracefully placed me down on my feet, well foot, when we got to the house.

'Why thank you Prince Charming!' I said jokingly with a smirk. He pecked me on the lips. Our faces were both dripping wet. I had hair in my eyes.

'You're welcome, princess.' He winked, then he carried me again up the stairs.

I thought I'd be nice and let Nathaniel decide which movie to watch.

'I loved your performance as Jasmine in Aladdin, she's one of my favourites,' he said.

I raised my eyebrows at him, 'What are you talking about?' It was safe to say I was confused.

'Just before when you were a princess, or do you need a refresher?' He laughed and said, 'My Jasmine, I can show you the world.' He thought he was being funny; I thought he had failed.

'Don't worry, Prince Charming, I enjoyed all of your roles in every single princess movie ever!' I teased.

It took him a while, but eventually Nathaniel pulled out a movie called 'Age of Adaline' and asked if I had seen it, which I had. He followed up by asking who she was.

'Well, you'd have to watch it to find out who she is.'

'No, I mean, who is Blake Lively? Her name sounds familiar.' He asked so innocently.

'I hope you're joking.' I deadpanned.

'No, I'm not.'

I widened my eyes and he saw my face. I shook my head.

'Tsk tsk tsk.' I sighed heavily 'Everyone should know who she is, but don't stress, I will teach you everything another day. Now we have no choice but to watch it. We have to start somewhere.'

We sat cuddled on the couch with the movie playing and whenever I looked at him, he seemed to be intensely focusing on the movie, which I found extremely adorable. He was routinely eating chips and having a sip of his drink. By the time the film had ended, as I personally predicted, Nathaniel let a few tears escape from his eyes. He was sniffling, trying not to start bawling too much.

'Aww, it will all be Okay!' I was rubbing his back, teasing him at the same time. I couldn't help but quietly laughing at him while wiping away his tears.

He gave me a little smack on the leg for laughing and then protested 'How are you not crying? Where is your heart?'

I continued to giggle at him. 'Well I've seen it before. I also tend not to cry in front of others, and I may have been watching you a little more than the movie. For what it's worth, it wasn't as upsetting as the movie.' I winked, then kissed him on the cheek to cheer him up.

'At least the you know the first Blake Lively movie you saw was good. Wait until we get to the others, not to mention 'Gossip Girl'.' He smiled at me, kissed me, and then excused himself to the bathroom to wash his face.

When Nathaniel came out of the shower, the redness in his eyes was still somewhat visible, as if he'd been crying more. 'Is everything all right?' I asked curiously.

He looked at me weirdly, 'Yeah, everything is fine, why?'

'Your eyes are red, just checking up.'

'Oh,' he chuckled lightly, 'no the movie just got me a little, it was such a cute story.' His cheeks started to darken with redness, I think I embarrassed him a little.

We had a bit of time to kill at the apartment, so we took the time to decide where to eat. I suggested a nice diner, not too far and casual and easy. In the meantime, Nathaniel got a phone call from Doctor Abrahms. She was checking up on him, and apparently, she was back early from her trip. I was told via Nathaniel that her orders were to treat him well. That lady was a very stern and blunt woman. He was smiling widely after the phone call. She always seemed to help lift his spirits, even if he wasn't feeling down.

We were both pretty hungry when we got to the diner. My stomach was singing for some food. By the time our food arrived, our appetites had reached astronomical levels. This place had mouth-watering burgers with such tasteful and delicious sauces. The smell coupled with our hunger made us both unable to eat in any manner which was mildly attractive. However, I teased that I was already his boyfriend, so it was fine. The first bite into the burger released one of the best foodgasms that I'd had all week. My satisfied moan after tasting the sauces explode into my mouth was very convincing. We were enjoying our food a lot, potentially a bit too much.

While snacking on the hot chips, we got to talking like we usually do. Since we still don't know all too much about each other, we always tried to learn something new about each other. Somehow, after the talk about my brother and his date, Nathaniel's week at work, and my time being at home, we got to the topic of our families.

I asked him about his because it had occurred to me that I didn't know much about his family at all.

I learnt that he only had one sibling, a brother who was a few years younger. I learnt that he didn't speak to his Dad, that he hadn't been around for the majority of his life. He told me his Mum had gotten really sick at one stage in her life, about four years back. Her kidneys had failed, and she was on dialysis for almost a year before she managed to get a transplant. At first, the doctors thought her body wasn't accepting the new kidney because she kept having reactions to it, but after a while everything quickly adjusted.

Nathaniel was quite shaken up from talking about it even now. I was happy to learn that his Mum happily remarried several years ago, and that Nathaniel had a close relationship with his brother and their stepfather. I realised in a passing thought that I had no idea when his birthday was. He told me it was the 8th of May, almost two months away. He proceeded to ask for mine, which was the 31st of January.

After that discussion, we went on to a more personal topic. He asked me about how things were when I came out to my family.

'Things were very strange for a while when I came out. My parents had sort of had a feeling and my brother had, too. So, one day, Mum asked me if I was and I told her the truth. She was very taken aback about the situation. She wanted me to have a wife and to give her grandchildren so, having that plan altered was jarring at first. She thought that I was breaking her heart and she really wanted to change the situation because she thought she was protecting me, but she was obviously unable to do so.

When the whole family found out at dinner after that, it made everything feel more real. Mum started to get upset, Dad was angry, and Zach was young, but old enough to understand what was happening. That was several years ago. It was tense for a short while after that and awkward at times. It made me want to get out of the house, but I was too young to live independently. Instead, I spent a lot of time out with friends, I didn't stay home much and when I did, I was in my room a lot, and that impacted on my relationship with my family. Most of all, on my relationship with my brother. I spent a lot less time with him because I didn't enjoy being at home, and whenever I was, I was either studying or playing games in my room which shut my brother out.

After some time, everything smoothed over and it was a lot less dramatic, I was home more, and we were closer as a family because of it. Now, things are better than ever, I only recently moved out, I'm only renting but it's affordable and I'm still able to save money.'

I assumed that Nathaniel was going to start with his own anecdote after I finished, but instead he asked a number of questions.

Did I have resentment? No. Was I angry about the way it was handled? I was a little angry. Did I have a boyfriend at the time? No.

'Wait, have you been in a relationship before?' he asked. He knew that I was still a virgin, but I guess he didn't know anything else about my love life, and to be fair, there wasn't too much to know.

'I've been in two relationships, neither of which were too recent, nor did they last too long. My first boyfriend was just after high school. We were young and in love, but he was in love with too many vices and I wasn't the type to deal with that, so I didn't. The second was about a year ago. It felt a bit more serious than the first, but we never ended up having sex because we never really got to that point in our relationship. Other situations took place but 'sealing the deal' as some would call it, was never completed. I've never been in a rush, so it doesn't bother me, it will happen when it happens.'

'Do you mind me asking what happened with the second boyfriend?' Nathaniel probed.

'We were just two very different people that couldn't merge into one union, it didn't work, and I think we both knew that early on, but we tried anyway.'

'So... I don't have to worry about anyone else showing up while we are together, right?' Nathaniel said, sounding very self-conscious.

'No, you don't have to worry, my only focus is you.' I said, smiling at him. His cheeks reddened as the words came out and then he leaned in and gave me a kiss, just a quick peck. I was still hesitant with the public displays of affection. He reached in for another kiss, but I cut him off.

'Nuh-uh, prince, I want to hear you story.' He raised his eyebrow at me after I pushed his lips away, then he started his account.

'Sure thing, well... to be honest, my family eased into it pretty quickly. Mum already had an idea that I was gay and even my little brother had thought I was several times but never said anything until after. I was 18 when I came out to the family and nobody really batted an eye. My step-dad was already forewarned by Mum.

His response was 'No shit, what's next? You're going to tell us you have brown hair?' which kind of shocked me because I was worried about telling them. I'd heard of so many scenarios where families would turn their backs on their own children. I was so thankful and grateful that my parents were as accepting as they were.

While I was worrying myself sick about everything, they had already known for ages and didn't even care. So yeah, that was my story, nothing intense.'

When Nathaniel finished talking, I sat there and stared him, smiling. He was very easy to listen to, mesmerising, and beautiful.

'What is it?' he said. At that point I think I got a little lost. I wasn't sure how long I had been staring for.

'I just enjoy hearing you talk, it's cute.' He smiled then as I was turning my head, he quickly pulled in and kissed me again.

'Can I do that again or are there more objections?' he teased.

'There are kids around! What if we're the reason they ask their Mummy why these two boys are kissing?'

Nathaniel laughed and said, 'Let us open their eyes at a young age.'

Without hesitation, Nathaniel continued to probe.

'Speaking of kids, you mentioned your mother wanted grandkids, were you still thinking about doing that?'

I choked a little. I wasn't expecting something like that to be asked this early.

'It's been like ten minutes of us being boyfriends and you're already asking about kids? The prince wastes no time! If you really want to know, yes, I'd like to have some, but the process is apparently very difficult and expensive. What are your thoughts?'

Nathaniel said, 'I don't mind, I'd like to have kids but I'm also aware that it might not happen.' His face turned very serious after that. He was looking me directly in the eye.

He said, 'Since I'm moving so fast, will you marry me?'

My eyes widened immensely and then Nathaniel started laughing really loudly.

'I was only joking. Your face was priceless!' He announced after calming down from the roars of laughter.

We kept talking for a while, ordered some sundaes for dessert and enjoyed each other's company. They say time flies when you're having fun, but apparently being in entertaining conversation has the same effect. It was almost three hours after we got there that we realised the time.

Before we got up to leave Nathaniel went to pay the bill, but the waiter told him it'd already been taken care of. I'd sneakily paid earlier when I 'went to the bathroom'. He was confused when the waiter denied him, so I told him that I'd paid. He was still confused as to when and how, but he was flustered and kissed me on the cheek before taking a breath.

On the drive home, I apologised for keeping him out until late, but Nathaniel said he was fine, he had an afternoon shift tomorrow. I asked if he wanted to stay the night. He got really excited, which made me happy. I never really had time to let it sink in that Nathaniel and I are more than just simply two guys going on dates. I'd have time soon to let reality catch up to me, but for now I wanted to live in the moment, so that's what I did.

When we got home, we watched a bit of TV before we got ready for bed. I gave Nathaniel a pair of my boxers to sleep in so that he would be more comfortable. He also mentioned that he wasn't planning for us to sleep in the same bed, because he didn't want to push anything.

I insisted though. I wanted to him to stay in the bed with me, and I didn't mind if it led to something.

So, he came and lay in the bed with me. We may not have hit any home runs, but we definitely reached some bases and got a little frisky before we slept, but once we did, it felt good to having someone sleep next to me. The sleep was peaceful and rejuvenating, until we heard a knock on the door the next morning.

CHAPTER 8

Moments

Nathaniel was shaking me awake. I shot up, asking what was wrong. I thought something was happening, and Nathaniel said someone was knocking on the front door. Barely even awake, I forced myself out of bed to check the door, hopping and dragging my way there.

It was Mum. She had food for me. I couldn't think of an excuse to leave her outside.

'Mum what the hell? What time is it?' I questioned.

'Jacob, it's almost 9:30 in the morning. You should already be awake. Anyway, I brought you some food, I'm not here to stay just dropping this off on my way to work.'

We made our way into the kitchen and Nathaniel, who was still in the bedroom, started coughing audibly. It scared the shit out of Mum.

'Jacob...what on Earth was that? Have you got company?' she asked, raising her eyebrow at me.

'Well umm, yeah I have a guy over… I think it might be too soon for you to meet him though, I'm just going to, quickly check up on him.' I hesitated.

'Not to worry Jacob, I'll leave you be.' She kissed me goodbye and I made my way back into the room.

As I walked into the room, I heard the front door close.

'So, I'm assuming you heard that conversation. My mum just came to drop off some food, but she heard you coughing from out there, meaning she'll be expecting to meet you some time soon. I think we're safe for now though.' I comforted him.

Nathaniel was sitting on the bed, looking somewhat relieved to have dodged a bullet. He got up and had nothing but his boxers on.

'Let's go have some coffee and breakfast.'

Nathaniel hopped out of bed and made his way to the kitchen, I followed him through, but I just needed to pee.

As I made my way to the kitchen, I heard Nathaniel talking but I told him I couldn't hear him.

When I stepped out, my Mum was sitting at the bench, with a sneaky looking smirk on her face.

'Hey Jacob, I decided not to leave just yet. I thought I would meet…' She turned her head towards Nathaniel, who was still in his boxers, and waited.

'I'm Nathaniel, Jacob's boyfriend, nice to meet you Mrs. Bartelli.' Nathaniel said, sounding like he was speaking through the nerves that rushed into his stomach.

Oh fuck, I thought…

My Mum looked up and down at Nathaniel, then she looked at me.

'Boyfriend?' she said. 'Jacob, where did you find this handsome gentleman and what is he doing here with you?'

Nathaniel blushed as he watched my mother pace towards me and smack me lightly on the back of the head.

'What the hell Jacob! First you refuse to tell me that you were in a stupid car accident and that you got hurt, and now you want to have a boyfriend without telling me? *And* you have the indecency and audacity to make Nathaniel be the one to tell me?'

'Mum, it's literally only been on…' There was no interrupting Mum.

'What else have you not told me? Have you joined the army? Have you got a second family? Robbed a bank, adopted a child?'

I thought she was finished.

'Mum, it has only been a day, we only became official yesterday and now here we are.' That will make her apologise.

'Oh, wait why would you have him meet me if it's only been a day? Jacob, you're going to scare him away if I haven't already.'

Then she spoke to Nathaniel.

'It was nice to meet you Nathaniel, regardless. Hopefully I'll get to see more of you, and if I don't, you probably made the right choice.' Mum snickered.

'MUM!' I yelled, trying to hint for her to head out of the door. Clearly she loved to stir the pot, the dramatics are all an act to show how much she cares. I honestly expect no less when it comes to my mother.

'Hey, I'm only joking, didn't you miss me? And you said you kept the accident a secret to keep me away.'

Then, Nathaniel decided to chime in with his response.

'For what it's worth, I told him to tell you what happened, but he didn't listen.'

I gasped and made a face at him, 'You snitch!'

Mum broke out in laughter, 'I like this guy Jacob, don't mess it up!' Then Mum grabbed her bag, said her goodbyes, and left the apartment, leaving Nathaniel and I alone.

Nathaniel spoke first, 'I don't know why I was so nervous; your mother was awesome, I love her already.'

I sighed heavily, maintaining a steady heartbeat, 'I'll be sure to let her know.'

We still had a couple of hours before Nathaniel had to leave for work, so we made some breakfast. After meeting Mum, Nathaniel was bubblier than ever. He couldn't sit still. He kept grabbing me and kissing me while I was trying to make pancakes. It felt great, don't get me wrong, but it was unexpected.

'Have you had a special drink or something? It's still early!' I teased.

He flashed me his signature smirk. 'No, I'm just happy, I realised something before.'

'What did you realise?' I quizzed.

'That you are actually my boyfriend.' He grabbed and kissed me again, but this time it wasn't a peck, it was slow and sensual, and the pancakes weren't the only thing heating up in the kitchen…

I had to break away, so the pancakes didn't burn. I had to admit, it felt good having someone, and it felt even better knowing that someone was Nathaniel. He was being cheesy. The kind that you think is gross when other couples do it, but it makes you feel things even though it's stupid. Some examples included:

'Is it hot in here or is it just you?'

'Where are your wings? Or did you have to parachute from heaven?'

'Do you think the pancakes would cook on your body or would they just burn?'

I had to stop him before he continued any longer, my goodness his jokes were so lame. The pancakes were done, and he was finally sitting down at the kitchen counter, slightly more relaxed but still a little hyperactive.

'Did you want some cheese on your pancakes with those cheesy ass lines?' He shot me a look as if to say, 'that wasn't funny at all'.

We ate slowly and gracefully, enjoying the food and each other. I was unintentionally observing his shirtless body and noticed a prominent birthmark slightly under his collar bone. I don't know how I never noticed it before, but it looked like a cute little paw print.

It felt as though so much had already happened today, but really it was only 10:30. Nathaniel still had over an hour before he'd have to leave. He kept looking around the apartment. I think he was just soaking everything in. Then he looked at me and started smiling as he was watching me eat. It was cute, but he didn't stop, so I put some chocolate sauce on my finger and poked it onto his nose. He shifted his head.

'Are we really doing this? You want to just make a mess of this beautiful breakfast that you made, only for you to lose huh?' He was teasing me, but I resisted the temptation to retaliate.

'You're very lucky Mr… wait, I just realised, I don't even know your last name. What is your last name?' I asked, surprised.

'Last name?' Nathaniel questioned. 'I'm too famous to have a last name, like Beyoncé or Rihanna, I just simply go by Nathaniel.'

I rolled my eyes at him.

'Do you want to just take mine? We've already dived into the deep waters, might as well keep going. You can just be Nathaniel Bartelli.'

Nathaniel chuckled, 'I actually don't mind the sound of that. My current last name, however, is Coren. Nathaniel Coren.'

'Mr Coren.' I couldn't remember what exactly we were talking about beforehand.

It was almost time for Nathaniel to leave, so he decided to have a shower before leaving. He looked at me.

'I'd invite you in,' he said. 'But I don't want to be late for work, maybe next time though.' He winked as he got up and went into the bathroom.

Nathaniel's shower was literally five minutes long, way too quick if you ask me. I barely managed to read three pages of my book before he was out. He had a towel wrapped around his body when he walked out. He was still dripping a little down his chest, and while he didn't have the most muscular build, his slim yet stern figure was stunning to look at. I couldn't stop staring at him as he walked to the room.

I stayed out in the lounge waiting. I didn't want to make him late for work. I really wanted to keep him here, but I knew I couldn't do that.

As Nathaniel was leaving for work, I kissed him before he got out of the apartment.

'Have a good day, tell Doctor Abrahms I said hello!'

He smiled and made his way to work.

Not long after, my phone started ringing. It was Zach. He had another date, and he wanted me to come over again to talk him through it, but also to hang out. He was going to pick me up, but I told him not to worry, I needed to walk, just to feel the fresh air. I got ready, made my way to the train station, and walked to Mum's after I got off the train and only Zach was home.

Thankfully so because I definitely wasn't ready to see mum just yet.

I helped calm Zach down. This was a more casual date than the first. I also helped him pick out an outfit, but he'd have to figure that out next time, otherwise she'd expect him to be up to my standards every time.

'Or, you could just confess to her that I helped you, if she asks.'

'Why on earth would I do that?' Zach questioned.

'So that she knows you're being honest, and she'd learn that you went out of your way to try and impress her.'

Mum got home before I managed to leave, which is exactly what I didn't want right now.

'Oh Jacob! I didn't expect to see you here, I thought you'd be with your boyfriend!'

That didn't take long at all… 'He had to go to work Mum.'

Zach overheard Mum and asked, 'Boyfriend? Is it Nathaniel?' he shouted with excitement.

Before I could even answer, Mum flared up and interrupted, 'So Zach already knew? Am I the only person who doesn't know? I'm glad at least someone in this family is up to date with your life. So, when is he coming to dinner?'

'Mum, not just yet! It's still a little early.'

'Yeah, I want to meet him as well.' Zach exclaimed. 'Maybe I can meet him before he comes for dinner, because that could be a while away.'

'Yeah, I will talk to him about it, it might be a little less overwhelming.' I smirked at Zach; it was strange but cute that he was so interested in my life. 'I'm assuming that Dad already knows?'

'Your mother told me in the car.' Dad announced as he entered the house, bringing the shopping inside with him. 'I don't want to be the only one who doesn't get to meet him.'

'Okay, Okay, I'll talk to him about dinner and see what he says, but don't be upset if he doesn't want to come for dinner in the next week. Anyway, I'm going!' I tried to get out of the house but then Mum asked where I was going. Apparently going home to rest meant that I was free to stay for dinner.

'You can always eat the food I brought you for lunch tomorrow. You're staying for dinner and I will drive you home afterwards.' Mum demanded.

So, without much choice, I stayed, and we ate dinner together as a family. Mum kept asking me questions about Nathaniel and then it clicked to me, I already told Mum about Nathaniel when they first came home! Accordingly, I confronted her, reminding her that I briefly told her about our date.

'Ha!' I yelled.

'Ha? Excuse me! You mean to tell me that you 'briefly' told me about a date right after a 20-hour flight *and* after I came home to see my son bandaged and in crutches, *and* you expected me to remember this ten second mention in passing conversation about a date?' She snapped, all sassy.

All I could do was laugh; I don't know why I even bothered trying to have one over Mum. She continued to ask questions about him, but I told her to stop, otherwise she would have nothing left to ask him when he comes over. I thought she was a little bit jealous, or maybe upset, that Zach knew more about Nathaniel than she did. However, realistically she was just being a nosy mother who wanted to pry as much as she possibly could and in an odd way, I appreciated it.

When we finished dinner, Mum drove me home early so that I could rest. We didn't speak too much on the drive home, but on my way out of the car she reminded me for the thousandth time to invite Nathaniel over for dinner soon.

By the time I got out of the shower, I was exhausted, but I couldn't get to sleep just yet. So, I put on a movie and lay down in bed, letting it play. I managed to shoot Nathaniel a message just saying that I hoped he had a good night, but I knew he wouldn't reply until later when he finished work. The television screen was still flashing with colours when I drifted off to sleep…

It was bright as ever when I woke up, the sun was glaring into my eyes and television was still on. My phone was buzzing, vibrating. Mum had messaged, asking if I needed anything, I told her I didn't, and then there was a message from Nathaniel. He said that I was to come to the hospital at 11:30 on Thursday to cut off my cast and to get my check-up. I'd have to get there on my own, but Nathaniel said he'd finish at 12 and that we could get lunch afterwards and he could take me home. Thursday arrived, and I caught a bus to the hospital. I messaged Nathaniel telling him I was here, but I think he was busy. I went to the lady at the desk.

'Someone will be here for you shortly,' she said. I only waited about two minutes before Doctor Abrahms came to get me.

'Hello Mr. Coren. I mean, Mr. Bartelli.' She winked. Before I could say anything, she continued, 'Don't worry,

I'm just teasing, I know you prefer Jacob. Come on, let's do this.'

Doctor Abrahms led me to a room and I followed her, looking for him. Then, when I was ordered to take the bed, I still had no sight of Nathaniel.

'Doctor Abrahms, are you doing all of this alone?'

She gave me a strange look and said, 'Well, obviously.'

'Sorry, I just meant…'

'He's had a bit of a rough day, I'm not entirely too sure why, he's just been in a weird mood. He did mention something about lunch, so I'll try not to keep you too long. Are you excited?'

'For lunch?' I asked. 'Yeah, I guess, I'm not too hungry but I always enjoy spending time with him.'

'That's great to hear, but I actually meant are you excited to get your cast off! We need to do some tests on your chest, just a quick, easy scan. I'd like to check your leg too, but it should be fine. Give me a moment to get the saw to cut it off.'

I knew it wasn't a tree-cutting saw, but I was still getting frightened.

When Doctor Abrahms returned, I think she saw it in my face.

'I promise it's not as scary as it looks,' she said. The whirring sound had started and instinctively, I flinched my leg, then held it still after Doctor Abrahms gave me a stern look. She started cutting into the cast but all I could think about was Nathaniel. I hoped he was Okay.

'So, after the cast comes off, I'm going to sponge it down. There will be a bit of dry skin and it might be a little discoloured but that will go back to normal in a day or two.'

It only took a couple of minutes to take the cast off, then I saw my leg and it had its colour back, but it was strange and carried a slightly sickening smell.

'Lucky, lunch might have been weird with a green leg. By the way, we need to have dinner together too, with Nathaniel preferably, but it's necessary with or without him. I still have my questions, nothing too probing but I'd like to get to know you on a more personal level.'

'I would be honoured and flattered to have dinner with you, after everything you've done for me it's honestly the least I could do.' I said sincerely.

'I'm looking forward to it. Now come on, we're going to walk to the other room to do a quick test.'

Doctor Abrahms grabbed me as I stood up and we walked to the room with the X-ray machine, without crutches. She held onto me for a short while and then let go and I could still walk all on my own. I could officially walk again! It definitely felt weird being back on two feet after finally getting used to the crutches. There was no pain, but I knew if I strained myself too much that it could possibly ache.

'Lay still Bartelli,' Doctor Abrahms announced. I guessed I wasn't completely cured yet.

About 15 minutes later, after laying down for the X-ray, Doctor Abrahms came back to the room and came to sit next to me.

'So, Jacob, I umm. I got the scans and from the look of it, everything is fine, except we found a bug inside you.'

'A *bug*?' I asked. I felt my heart racing.

'Yes!' she placed her hand over my heart and said, 'the love bug.' She instantly started laughing after delivering her joke. 'I'm sorry, I had to. Everything is fine, you're doing fine and there is nothing at all to worry about.'

'Oh my God, you gave me a scare. Can't I sue you for that?'

Doctor Abrahms shot me the fiercest look.

'Do it, I dare you,' she said sternly. Then she burst into laughter again. 'Go enjoy your lunch and please try to cheer Nathaniel up. He's waiting in the lobby.'

'Thank you so much for everything, Doctor Abrahms. I'll let Nathaniel know that we need to have dinner together and if he can't make it, we'll go, just the two of us.'

She smiled on my way out.

'You can call me Victoria,' she said.

I met Nathaniel downstairs in the lobby. He was standing near the exit, looking gloomy. When he looked at me, I ran to him and hugged him tightly.

'Look! I can walk again. I can run!' I picked him up and ran outside carrying him. I wasn't as strong as he was, but I was still capable. When I put him down outside, my shoulder was a little sore and my leg informed me instantly that I should hold off before doing that again. Nathaniel cracked a smile, which made me jump into him and kiss him.

He still seemed upset, but I didn't bring it up. I was really happy and excited, so I thought I'd try to spread some of that excitement to him. I thought I would wait until lunch to ask him about his day.

'So, can I ask where we're going for lunch?'

'You can't stay still,' Nathaniel chuckled at me. 'We're just going to a cute café around the block.'

'Around the block? And you want to drive? Can't we walk? I can walk now! I'll give you a piggyback if you like!' I tried to plead.

'Definitely not! I can't be bothered walking. I'm feeling tired, sorry. You should also still be taking it easy for a little while. You shouldn't have lifted me up earlier. I don't want you to injure yourself again before you've recovered. It was cute though.' Nathaniel leaned in and pecked me on the lips.

We drove to the café, sat down, and ate. As much as I tried, Nathaniel still seemed a little distracted and tense.

'Nathaniel, tell me what's wrong?'

'What do you mean? I'm fine,' he responded.

'Nathaniel, it started when I noticed you weren't at the hospital when I arrived, which is fine, but when I asked Doctor Abrahms, she mentioned it to me. Then, when I finally got to see you, you seemed down. What's wrong? I'm worried.'

He lifted his head, sighed and said, 'It's stupid. I had a weird day at work, nothing bad. I just kept thinking about us.' He seemed defeated.

'About us? What were you thinking about?'

'Well, I was excited at first, that you were getting your cast cut off. Then, I thought that maybe you wouldn't want to be with me anymore. You don't really need me anymore so I just thought, why would he stay?' He looked down and realised he was being stupid, but everyone has their own insecurities.

'Nathaniel don't be silly! Being injured, having you help me out through this whole thing in the way that you have, I absolutely appreciate that. However, that's not at all the reason that I like you. You're hilarious, caring, thoughtful, kind, beautiful, and sexy. I could keep going if you'd like. And if anything, it means that now I can do things a lot easier, we can do more things together.' I tried my best to convince him but sometimes actions do speak louder than words.

Before he could rebut me, I grabbed him, drew him towards me and pressed my lips into his, giving him my love and affection through a kiss. When we pulled apart, he smiled gracefully.

'Thank you for that,' he said. His mood seemed to brighten up from then on.

'Oh, by the way, if you wanted to make this feel more real and serious, my mother is upset because she only briefly got to meet you and would love to have dinner. I know it's still pretty soon and all, but she wants to invite you to meet you properly. I told her I'd speak to you, well ask you, but that it's still a little early. Zach is also extremely excited to meet you, probably on our own, without Mum and Dad first. And before I forget, Doctor Abrahms also wanted to have dinner with me, regardless of whether you come, but I think I'd prefer that you came.' I was exhausted just thinking about all of these meetings.

Nathaniel's smile expanded immensely.

'So, you're telling me that we've already got two dinners to plan and that your brother wants to meet me… maybe I should get out while I still can,' he mocked me with laughter. 'When is dinner with your family? I can do Sunday night if that works, although if that's too soon we can find another time. Would your brother be able to hang out tonight? Maybe we could do something that he enjoys.' Nathaniel seemed excited.

'This might be weird, but would I also be able to meet your family? It only seems fair to your family and to you. I'll also ask Zach about tonight and see if he's free.' Nathaniel seemed a little taken aback by my request.

'Yeah, I mean if you are ready then why not? This is all a tad extremely fast, it's been less than one week since our talk, but I'm down if you are.' Nathaniel wasn't hesitating, but I was starting to get very nervous. I don't know how well it works when people jump straight into relationships, I guess I'll find out soon.

'Oh, I guess so. Maybe you're right. Nathaniel, if you don't want to have dinner with our families yet, we can push it back until we are ready. It's no harm, we can spend time with each other instead first.'

Nathaniel laughed at me, 'We can do both, we might as well get it over with, then we can have a break from them for a while. Let's start with your brother.'

CHAPTER 9

Two Families in Four Nights

Thursday Night

Zach was free and so were Nathaniel and I, so I told him to meet us back at the apartment. I had to have a shower when we got back home, however Zach had already arrived. The skin that had been under the cast was getting very itchy and I felt uncomfortable. Plus, I thought it would be better for them to talk for a bit without me. When I introduced them to each other, Zach was still super excited and when I ducked out to shower, it was like they didn't even notice. When I got out of the shower, they were talking and laughing with each other. I didn't know whether to feel happy or jealous.

'What are you guys laughing at?'

'Nothing of your concern.' Zach winked. They already had inside jokes.

We decided to order some takeaway and have a game night. Zach didn't want anything fancy and he wanted to talk and get to spend time with us more than anything. So, we ordered some burgers and played some board games and trivia games.

In the meantime, the questions were flying back and forth, not just the trivia ones. Turns out they're both nerds, I mean I am too, but they read the same books, play similar video games and are both into sci-fi, Star Trek Wars or something.

'Hold on a second, am I... dating my brother?' I asked out loud.

Zach laughed and teased me.

'You missed me too much and couldn't live without me.'

'That's a little creepy, Jacob!' Nathaniel teased, nudging me. I didn't know what to feel other than awkward.

As the night went on, things ran smoothly, Nathaniel and Zach were connecting, legitimately bonding. It made me glad to see that they were so comfortable with each other so quickly. I told Zach that we were going to ask Mum to do dinner on Sunday.

'If you're going to come for dinner on Sunday, why did you invite me over tonight?' Zach asked, not in an annoyed manner, but in a curious tone.

'Well you said you wanted to meet him before the dinner, so I thought you'd want to catch up and meet him tonight.'

Zach's smile widened. 'Oh really? Jacob, you know you didn't have to do that, I would have been fine with Sunday alone, but thank you.'

'Yeah, I know, but we were also celebrating my ability to walk again. It worked out for both of us, all three of us, actually.' I was happy to know that Zach was so pleased and excited to spend time with us.

Nathaniel had been unintentionally cut out of the conversation, so I brought him back into it.

'Nathaniel, has Zach warned you about how Sunday might turn out?' I teased.

Sunday Night

Tonight was the night of the family dinner at my parents' house. Nathaniel just got to my apartment, after he finished work, and he wanted me to prepare him for my family. When he walked out of the shower, he, once again, left me speechless. Something about the wet hair, the water dripping from his body, and his pretty face just made my heart race faster.

'Stop staring at me like that you perve! I can feel you undressing me with your eyes and I'm only wearing a towel! We have serious business to go over.' Nathaniel was getting very nervous which was making me feel nervous, even though I knew it would be fine.

He got dressed and sat down on the bed, and we discussed the questions that might be asked. I tried to calm him down and massaged him gently so that he could relax. He was slowly easing down, and then it was my turn to get dressed and ready before we leave.

When I finished my shower and got dressed, Nathaniel was chilled and ready to go. Now I was the one who was nervous, for my family not to embarrass me and for them not to scare Nathaniel. We also decided that I would be driving, this is my first time driving since the accident…

As soon as we got into the car, fear ran right through my body and I didn't want to move. I don't know how long I froze for, but it was Nathaniel who eventually thawed me out. He grabbed my hand and I think he knew what was happening because he asked if it was still too soon for me to drive. I told him that I needed to force myself and get it over and done with. I insisted that maybe I should just go around the block first without him in the car in case anything happened, but he didn't hesitate or budge. It was also my first time driving this car. Dad thought it ran well but I needed some time to be comfortable with it.

'Listen, you just breathe, drive slow if you aren't comfortable and we will just take our time. We can put the music low and enjoy the drive, but I'm not going anywhere, we're doing this together.' He said calmly, it was oddly soothing. The way he spoke and the way he comforted me really helped to ease my mind. It didn't have to be a big deal if I didn't make it one.

I turned the car on, and my anxiety was starting to creep up on me, but then having Nathaniel with me made me feel braced and steady. I had to force myself to focus because I wasn't just responsible for myself in the car, I couldn't have anything happen to him. I was a little edgy at first, but after the first couple of minutes it all started to feel normal again. It will always be at the back of my mind, maybe a little more prominently for now, but people have accidents all the time and I couldn't let it control my life.

My heart was pounding, and I was sweating by the time I got my parents' house, a mixture of nerves about the dinner and relief from driving to Mum's safely. I needed a minute to gather myself. One hurdle down and now it was time to face the next. We gave each other a look. Nathaniel finally seemed confident when he looked back at me; hopefully that oozed off onto me as well.

I pressed on the doorbell and waited for someone to answer. Within seconds, Mum opened to door with a huge grin on her face. She hugged Nathaniel with a kiss on each cheek, then she looked at me and said her greetings, giving me the same kisses.

I introduced Mum and Nathaniel to each other even though they'd already met. Mum raised her brow at me.

'Jacob, you realise we've already met, and we know each other's names.' Nathaniel still referred to her as Mrs. Bartelli rather than as Juliet.

When I brought Nathaniel into the dining room, Zach and Dad were sitting down waiting. 'Nathaniel, you already know Zach, and this is my dad Anthony, Dad this is my boyfriend Nathaniel.'

Dad got up and shook Nathaniel's hand while Zach got up and gave us both a hug. They both seemed like they were in a good mood. Nathaniel went to the kitchen to see if Mum wanted help with dinner. That definitely got him some brownie points, Mum yelled from the kitchen.

'Thank you Nathaniel! Maybe next time your boyfriend and his brother would get off their behinds and help out instead of having our guest be the one to offer to help.'

My brother and I received an extremely stern and terrifying look from Mum when herself and Nathaniel started bringing out the food. I got up to try and help set the table, but Mum rejected my offer.

'It's too late now, don't try to redeem yourself.'

Nathaniel and Mum finished bringing the food and setting up the table. They both sat down to join the family. It almost felt like I was the one who had to please Mum, rather than Nathaniel. Not too long into dinner, Dad started asking Nathaniel questions, nothing interrogatory, just getting to know him and what he did for work. Mum already knew all this about Nathaniel and so did Zach.

Surprisingly enough, everybody behaved at dinner.

Everybody was talking and keeping the conversation going, getting to know Nathaniel. It started to feel a little more intense when the questions started to get a little deeper.

'So, is this something you guys think will last or…' Dad asked jokingly, but it struck a nerve.

'Dad! We're just trying to figure things out and we are getting to know each other.'

Then Mum tried to joke a little, 'So, does that mean kids are still in the question?'

'Yeah, I'm pregnant right now with triplets and there are four more on the way! Honestly though, you guys can relax with the questions. We are going with the flow and enjoying each other's company. We know it's early, but you wanted me to invite him because you thought I was hiding something.'

The room was silent after I finished speaking and surprisingly, Nathaniel resumed the conversation by asking about their holiday.

They were happy talking about it and were somewhat appreciative of me not worrying them with my accident.

'He was clearly in good hands anyway.' Mum winked at Nathaniel and I could feel my body cringing, but Nathaniel was laughing. 'Have you been feeling any pain since the accident?'

'I've had a couple physical incidences where I feel like I need to sit down for a moment and rest, but the mentality of getting back into a car took me a moment. Even now I still shudder more than I used to, especially when I'm watching from the passenger seat and don't have the same control.' I admitted honestly. I did not want to worry my mother, but I also was not planning to lie to her again.

It felt a little strange watching everything around me. I became an observer in that moment while Nathaniel was talking to my family. Was this all happening too fast? It had only been under a week even though technically we'd been dating for a while. Did I have doubts about Nathaniel? No. I know I did have doubts, but I know that I have feelings for him. I just thought that everything might have been going a lot quicker than usual relationships. Then again, what did it matter if we were doing things differently? We didn't have to compare ourselves to other people. The important thing at the end of the day was that we were happy with each other. Even if we rushed into everything, this was something that we decided to do together. Now we just had to take the plunge and see how it went. Hope for the best and put our effort in to make it work.

When I zoned back into the conversation, they were all looking at me as if they were waiting for me to reply. Before I could ask what they had said, Nathaniel filled me in.

'Jacob, your parents asked what you thought when you first saw me.' Then Nathaniel started chuckling lightly.

I remember I was a little drugged up when I first saw Nathaniel and I was also being a little cocky if I remember correctly.

'I think I was pretty excited with what I saw.'

'Actually, as soon as I walked through the door your son was very honest with what he was thinking because it flowed right out of his mouth with no filter. He was very confident but there was a fair amount of medication flowing through his body at that point.'

All four of them started laughing and I could feel my face blushing from embarrassment. I had no other choice but to join them in laughter. 'That is very true, I paid a lot of attention to the smirk that he makes, it is very cute. I was also drawn in by his colourful green eyes.'

The night continued in the same manner. The family kept talking to both me and Nathaniel. We finally left the house and went back into the car to drive home.

'I thought that went pretty well, it seemed like they enjoyed our company and they weren't anywhere near as invasive as you made them out to be.'

'Yeah that honestly went a lot smoother than I thought it would go. Hopefully the same thing happens in the next two dinners, especially with your family.' I could tell that mum was trying to impress me by trying to be open. I knew it was not something that she was used to, but I certainly appreciated her for trying. I would also bet that she had a word to my father about behaving. They have honestly come a long way from where they used to be, they never thought that this would be a part of their world and their growth makes me so happy.

I was glad that my family were welcoming to Nathaniel. Now the tables were turned, and I was in the position to try to impress Doctor Abrahms and Nathaniel's family. Even thinking about it was making my body churn with nerves. This was going to be difficult.

Wednesday Night

Nathaniel was more nervous to have dinner with Doctor Abrahms. He said that she had been acting really strange ever since she came back from her holiday. She was more reserved and quieter. Something seemed off and Nathaniel was hoping that she would be all right. His nerves were starting to worry me, and I kept trying to calm him down, although it wasn't really working. I told him that I was under the impression that she just wanted to get to know me more.

I had to drive just so that Nathaniel could relax. I still felt weird driving, it no longer felt like it was second nature to me. I was still nervous about driving but it was something I knew would eventually diminish.

We were headed to a funky little restaurant that wasn't too far away. By the time we arrived at dinner, Nathaniel had seemed to calm down. Doctor Abrahms hadn't arrived yet so we waited at our table.

'Hey, why are you so nervous? I'm sure everything will go smoothly.' I kept rubbing Nathaniel's knee to try and comfort him, but I could tell it wasn't working. I thought he calmed down before, but he was still extremely fidgety.

He was very serious when he replied, 'She just means a lot to me and for some reason something just seems, different. I can tell that something is up, I just can't figure out what it is.'

'Babe, I know that she's a very important person in your life and I understand completely that you're nervous, but I've already met her several times.' I felt like Nathaniel just needed to take a few deep breaths, or maybe something else…

'Excuse me sir!' I called the waiter and ordered another drink for Nathaniel since I was the one driving for the night.

We only sat alone for about ten minutes or so before Doctor Abrahms arrived. We both got up to greet her as soon as we saw her and as we did, Nathaniel managed to bump the table and knocked over the table water, spilling quite a lot of it on the tabletop. Doctor Abrahms laughed, teasing Nathaniel.

'Someone is excited to see me.' Almost the moment they interacted; Nathaniel instantly reverted and became comfortable and calm. It made me jealous to see that Victoria had the power to suddenly make Nathaniel feel at ease. On the other hand, I was here struggling to even distract him from worrying, but it also made me realise why I respected her so much.

After we ordered our food, the talking started, just small talk about life and work and the past couple of nights. I was trying to read her emotions and her body language because of what Nathaniel was saying earlier, but I personally didn't really notice anything too different. The restaurant was quite busy, which usually meant that the food is worth waiting for.

Doctor Abrahms asked how I was going after getting the cast off, she also made sure I call her Victoria, so I did. After that, she asked if I was comfortable with the driving.

'You told her?' I looked at Nathaniel, I wasn't angry, but I did feel kind of embarrassed.

'No, I didn't say anything.' He reached for my leg under the table and gently squeezed my thigh. I think that he was now trying to make me feel relaxed.

'I just asked because it's common for people to struggle after an accident. Everything's Okay now?' Victoria asked. I told her about my panicked moment. She'd predicted something like that would happen. I supposed she would know most of these things considering her work.

Not too long after, the food started to come out and my stomach was ready to eat. It was a beautifully cooked steak for me, medium rare with no blood, and it smelled as delicious as it tasted. My stomach was more than satisfied after I finished my meal. The other two were still slowly eating the rest of their meals. It wasn't until Victoria finished eating that the questions started to come up again.

'So, time to get to the real stuff. Jacob, you're a great guy, you already know that I like you and you already know that Nathaniel has become somewhat like a son to me. With that being said, it's my turn to grill you,' she smirked at me with a teasing look. 'Nothing too intense, I know it isn't my relationship, but I guess I just would like to know your intentions are and how serious you are about Nathaniel. It might be out of my place, but I have my reasons.'

I took a long sip of my drink before I answered her question, but really it was an easy one.

'Well, I'm happy with how we are getting along with each other. I know it all seems like we've rushed into it all a bit too quickly, but if anything, it just goes to show how seriously I feel about Nathaniel. It also does not feel rushed in the slightest bit, at least not for me. I'm generally not the kind of person who needs to experiment with a number of people before I settle down. I really do like Nathaniel and I'm ready to put in the effort to make it work.' I smiled at Nathaniel. His face started to blush a little.

Victoria started smiling, she seemed extremely happy.

'I'm glad to hear it. What about you Nathaniel?' She turned her head and focused her attention on Nathaniel. 'How do you feel about the situation and about Jacob?'

Nathaniel made a face; he was visibly taken aback by the question. I don't think he expected Victoria to question him.

'Ahh, uhm... Well, I really like Jacob too, I'm still a little scared because of my previous relationships, but this just feels different. It feels effortless with Jacob and I really admire that. Things just work, the way we connect is something that I usually have to try and create. I'm just as serious about this as he is when it comes to relationships and we've already spoken to each other about it. We're both on the same page and we have already been through so much in the last few weeks and it's already forced us to grow as a couple. In a weird way, I'm very much grateful for it.' Listening to Nathaniel talk about us made me feel warm, happy, and assured.

Victoria was absorbing what both Nathaniel and I had said, and she seemed content with where we were in our relationship. It felt a little strange that Victoria would be questioning us, but I assumed that maybe it was her way of trying to protect Nathaniel. I reached for Nathaniel's hand under the table when we finished talking. At this point, all I wanted to do was jump over the table and kiss him, but that would be a tad inappropriate. Personal displays of affection made me feel weird anyway, especially being gay. It didn't take long for the dessert to come and both Victoria and Nathaniel had been drinking a little bit.

Halfway into dessert, Victoria let out a heavy sigh.

'So, I have something important that I need to tell you.' There was a moment of silence before anything else came out. 'Well, I'm pregnant…'

She started to tear up and when Nathaniel tried to get up, Victoria put her hand up to stop him.

'Let me finish.' I tried to say congratulations, but she kept on going, her voice was weak, and she was starting to choke up when she continued. 'I took a pregnancy test and then, I went to the doctor to get an ultrasound. When I was at the doctor, I noticed a lump on the bottom of my breast, and I wasn't too sure what it was.' Nathaniel was frozen and he had tightened his hand firmly into mine.

'As you probably figured, we ran tests on the lump, and it came back positive for breast cancer. It's still early stages and very much manageable.' She sounded firm and stern again, almost as if she was reassuring a patient. My heart went out to her. I couldn't imagine how she was feeling. She was pregnant *and* she figured out she has breast cancer; I didn't know what to do. Nathaniel got up and hugged her, she tried to refuse it, but he persisted through, just like Victoria will.

'What's the treatment for it at this stage? Do you need anything from us? Are you still going to work for now?' Nathaniel had a million more questions, but he also needed to breathe and let everything sink in.

'The treatment at the moment is just surgeries to remove the lumps. Any chemo-therapy at this stage will most likely affect the baby so we're trying to wait as long as possible. It's a lot safer for the baby after the first trimester and I'm only two months along. Here is the issue though, while the cancer is extremely frightening and scary, from a doctor's perspective, I have pretty good odds and the cancer isn't too dangerous.

I only have a month before the treatment, and I'll be under close eye just in case I need to start the chemotherapy earlier. Myself and my husband Greg have been discussing it all, we've never really wanted to have a baby and we still don't, so this all came as a surprise. We're still young and so we have to decide whether or not to terminate the pregnancy before it gets too late. It would also help for me to focus on the cancer.'

There was a strong silence after Victoria spoke. Her situation was tremendously heartbreaking, but she was full throttle about it. I have no idea how she'd managed to still be so calm and organised about everything. It was clear that her confidence influenced both Nathaniel and I because it was the only thing keeping us both from breaking down right now, forcing us to be calm and serious about this entire situation. I didn't really understand why Victoria wanted to keep the baby if she didn't want to raise it, but maybe deep down she did want a baby.

Nathaniel spoke. 'No matter what you decide to do, we support you one hundred per cent. I think it's very brave of you to be here discussing it with us. Nobody will be judging you because of your decisions, it's your right to do whatever you like with your body. Jacob and I will be here if you ever need anything.' Nathaniel didn't hesitate to start comforting Victoria. I completely agreed with everything that he said.

Victoria took a moment to down her drink, which I now realised was water. Then, she had more to share with us.

'Well, before the night ends, I want to give you both a proposition. I already spoke with Greg about our options, as you know, and we came to another possible conclusion. Greg didn't think it would be the best idea right now, but I wouldn't be able to sleep properly if I didn't ask. Nathaniel, I know this is an extremely huge ask, but I wanted to go through with the pregnancy so that I could give the baby up for adoption, more specifically, for you to adopt.'

I felt my eyes widen with surprise and I saw Nathaniel's jaw drop to the floor. We were both frozen with shock, I couldn't comprehend what had just happened. Victoria noticed our reactions and then continued.

'I know it's extremely early in your relationship, so of course there is absolutely no pressure on what you decide to do, but it's an opportunity for the both of you. The only issue is, you have got less than a month to make this decision, and even though you guys are both still young, I know Nathaniel has spoken about children before, so this is entirely your decision. Regardless of what you decide to do, this isn't a favour to me and it won't impact on my cancer, so don't let that affect your judgement. I think it's important that you both discuss everything as a couple and talk about what you want to do. I know it seems odd, but I have always been so focused on my career and achieving my personal goals that I never intended to have children. Even now, being pregnant, I still don't want to have a child to raise. However, I have always wanted to know what birthing a child would feel like, so think of this as another milestone in my life and my way of giving something back to the universe. My mind is made up, the rest if up to you.'

CHAPTER 10

The Talk

I think it's safe to say that the night ended very differently to how we had expected it to end. Dinner was over and I think we were all a little tense and emotional about the situation. The drive home with Nathaniel was the quietest drive we've ever had together. Nathaniel was looking out the window for most of the drive home and I could physically see him fighting back the tears. I reached over and held his hand with one of mine while I had the other on the steering wheel. It wasn't until we got back to the apartment that we both sat on the couch and started to talk.

'Jacob…' Nathaniel started off, heavy and serious. 'I don't know what to do. I'm so scared for her because what if something happens? What if we decide something and then Victoria ends up…'?

'Stop Nathaniel, you can't think like that, Victoria is giving you an opportunity and it's up to you to decide. The only drawback is that she would have to hold back on the chemotherapy until the baby has reached its first trimester. At the same time, if you go through with this, Victoria will be going through a pregnancy while simultaneously battling cancer and that is a lot for anybody to take on. It's difficult for us, well for you, to make a decision that may impact on her health and life. Take away the cancer from the equation for just a moment Nathaniel, not to sound selfish but just to help figure out your mind. If there was no cancer to consider, at this point in your life, would you want to take on a baby?' I had to break things down in order to try and put things in perspective and at least get some sort of answer into this situation.

'If I wasn't putting anybody at risk, I think I would take the opportunity because it's something that is so rare. This isn't something that pops up whenever. We would usually have to plan and spend a lot of money and time in doing this. I know we're not there yet though; I still have to consider us as a relationship, and we can't be selfish and disregard the fact that it would be a weight on Victoria. And Jacob, this doesn't only affect me, you have a say too. What do you think about it all?'

'Honestly, this would be a blessing that definitely doesn't come often, that's for sure. We do have to consider the fact that it's still Victoria's body and we obviously don't want to put her in any greater risk. In regard to our relationship, it is still very fresh, but it's been almost a month, right? If we include our time together at the hospital, then we've known each other for a short while. We still are new to each other, yes, but that does not necessarily mean it is a bad thing. People raise children after a one-night stand, and this is a very different situation to that. The worst-case scenario is that we have a falling out and you're left raising the baby on your own. Of course, that isn't out goal or anything, but you should think realistically here. If something does happen, will you be still willing to raise a baby?' I wasn't trying to curse our relationship or anything, but I was just trying to be realistic and have Nathaniel understand the seriousness of this situation.

'So... does that mean you don't want to have a child? Or are you saying that you might not be here to stick around with me?' He started to sound worried.

'I'm not saying that at all. I'd absolutely love to have this opportunity with you, but this is a curveball thrown by a machine at 300 miles per hour and we have to decide whether to swing or let it go. And if we swing, we might hit a home run, or we might strike out. I just want you to be ready in case we strike out.' I had to be honest about the situation because there is no telling what might happen in the future.

Nathaniel seemed extremely torn. 'I suppose you're right, but I need to know one thing. If I do decide to do this, is it going to push you away? I know it's really early in our relationship, so I don't want to jeopardise that either.'

'I will be here to see where we end up either way. I've honestly never been happier in my life and I think a baby would be an absolute miracle. In saying that, there is no denying the level of stress and impact that this will inflict onto our relationship. I think you need to sleep on it, then discuss it more deeply with Victoria and see whether or not she really wants to do this. From my end, I'm completely all in and ready for whatever you decide. I know Victoria is a strong, grown ass woman but I think she also needs to understand what risks she might be undertaking.'

'Alright.' Nathaniel said reluctantly, then with a little more excitement he said, 'I think we can definitely have another if not many more conversations with her about it.'

'Absolutely. I also think that we need to have more conversations too. Don't get me wrong Nathaniel, I want to be with you and I want to do this, but I would be lying if I said I wasn't scared. I don't even know you all that much and to be honest, I think you could very well say the same about me.' I couldn't ignore the obvious in this situation.

'You're right, there is no way to guarantee that this will work out. I do know that I am happy with you by my side and I want to continue to get to know you. I also know that if we do this, we still have several months before this baby arrives. I know this will fast track our entire relationship, so we have to be in total agreeance on this. I don't know if we're ready for a child, individually or as a united front, but I know that personally, I will very much be able to get ready and step up.' Nathaniel spoke from his heart.

'I feel the same way. I will be able to step up because this is something that I have always wanted, I suppose I just didn't think it would have this soon in my life or in my relationship with someone. However, for now I agree that we should take this opportunity while we can. I still want us to talk to Victoria about this more thoroughly.' Jacob said his peace and Nathaniel agreed with a large smile on his face.

We opened up a bottle of champagne to have a celebratory glass and to help us wind down before bed.

'Do you still want to go to family dinner on Friday?'

'I think we definitely need to have that dinner, especially now, but I'm not sure if you should bring up the baby news yet. We'll have to see how the night turns out. It will be your mother, step-father and brother, right?' Thinking about it made me nervous.

'Yes, hopefully it's a nice and relaxing evening.' Nathaniel was growing tired and he had work the next day, so, we decided to head to sleep. It took him about two minutes to fall asleep, I stayed awake reading for a while before I eventually fell asleep too.

Nathaniel was already having a shower when I woke up. He was tossing and turning a lot last night; I don't think that he had gotten the best sleep. Mine was a little shaky too but my stomach was stopping me from going back to sleep, as it was clearly breakfast time.

We didn't get much time together in the morning because Nathaniel had to head to work. He was also going to speak with Victoria about the situation, just to make sure that Victoria was completely aware of what she was doing. We've decided that, even though it's a little early, we would be absolutely honoured and grateful to be able take this opportunity. Raising a baby will be one of the hardest things we ever do, possibly alongside keeping this relationship afloat. While I was at home, I still had more restaurant reviews to write for work, but next week I'd be able to head back to work full time. I was even thinking of doing overtime or even a job on the side to try and got more income. There were plenty of inspections around the city the needed to be completed.

By the time I had finished going over the reviews that I had written it was almost 3pm, so I spent a bit of time looking at cots online and the excitement just took over me. It was like it all hit me that we might actually be having a baby that we could raise. I wanted to have this baby a lot more than I initially thought I did, but I didn't want to get too excited because there was no guarantee that this situation was going to work out.

However, it was very difficult to contain the excitement.

When Nathaniel came back to the apartment, he woke me up. I had fallen asleep with the laptop in my hands while I was still laying on the couch. He'd seen what I was looking at and then he smiled and kissed me, even though I was groggy from my nap. Nathaniel squeezed me over and came to sit next to me. He had a big smile on his face, so I was pretty sure I knew what he was going to say. He grabbed my leg.

'So, I had a serious talk with Victoria,' he said. 'We spoke for quite a while and she said that she is still more than happy to do this for us. I told her that we would be honoured and that regardless of what happens from here on out, she needs to put herself first. So, I guess we are having a baby?!' Nathaniel shrieked. He was smiling from ear to ear, and then I screamed out of happiness. Then he grabbed the back of my head and pulled my face towards his, clashing our lips together through our smiles.

It started to get very heated and Nathaniel pulled back, but then I pushed into him. We were literally going to raise a baby together in about six months' time. I was definitely ready for us to keep going and take the next step in our relationship. Nathaniel pulled back again and raised his eyebrow as if to ask if I was sure, and I was. He pulled my head towards his and we started off slow, letting our emotions take control of our bodies. Nathaniel was a little reluctant at first, he kept trying to make sure that I was comfortable and that I was certain.

I was, but I quickly ducked out to the bathroom, just to make sure that everything was… clean. I came back, and he was smiling at me, waiting for me to come back into his arms, and without any pressure or discomfort, I did exactly that. I felt extremely lucky to be with someone who truly cared for me. We were in each other's arms and one thing was leading to another. First, we were just making out with each other, caressing one another and before we knew it, we were getting friskier. Our bare skin was touching and pressing against each other while we were making love.

When we finished, surprisingly, my first-time having sex wasn't as bad as people made out it would be. The whole process was strange, but he made me feel extremely comfortable and then we just flowed into each other. I had watched enough 'content' to know what to do, although it took a moment to get used to everything, but it all felt right. It's safe to say that Nathaniel is packing. In addition to that, I thought I was falling in love with him…

Afterwards, we just lay next to one another for a while on the bed, talking and cuddling. My mind was going all over the place. I was thinking about everything that had just happened, thinking about whether or not I loved Nathaniel and thinking about the fact that we hopefully would have a baby with us in the next six to seven months or so.

I didn't know if anybody else's relationship moved this fast, but I felt like so much had happened in the last couple of months. My life had always been quiet, simple, and somewhat stagnant; however, this has probably been the most progression I've had in such a short amount of time. It was weird to think that we'd be raising a baby soon.

We were resting on the bed, but the peaceful silence was broken by the sound of Nathaniel's stomach rumbling. We cleaned up and then we ordered some food. He put a movie to relax and wait for the food to arrive. He seemed really stressed about family dinner, with his Mum specifically. We'll just have to wait and see what happens.

CHAPTER 11

Sticking to the Plan

My stomach was aching from the nerves when Nathaniel rang the doorbell to his mother's house. Nathaniel put his arm around my back. At first it made me jump, but then it seemed to calm me for moment, until I heard the doorknob twist. The door swung open and Nathaniel's mother was smiling wide. She was extremely welcoming, hugging us both and then leading us into the dining room. Nathaniel's little brother and his stepfather were sitting at the dining table, ready to eat.

Nathaniel introduced me to his family before we took our seats. His mother Marissa, stepfather Stefan and brother Mitchel were all very attractive and were also exceptionally welcoming. I could almost immediately feel their warmth as if it was a permeating aura. Marissa insisted that we take our seats and so we did. The smell from the kitchen had made its way to the table, as did the source of the aroma.

The beef casserole was absolutely delicious and Mrs Williams, who insisted I called her Marissa, was very excited and happy to be meeting me. She was very gracious and loving. Her was curly and it was bouncing as she walked, it made her cute aesthetic complete and assisted in delivering her bubbly personality.

A few questions started to fly my way, but she was just getting to know me. She asked how we met because apparently Nathaniel hadn't told her too much. When I told her the entire story her facial expressions were changing from worry to sympathy and then from happiness to delight as I recounted the time at the hospital.

She said she remembered Nathaniel mentioning something about one of his patients a couple of months back being flirty with him and lightening up his day.

Nathaniel's stepfather Stefan, on the other hand, didn't talk too much. He seemed a little timid, but after learning what I did for work, he started to open up more. He worked as a chef and he'd been at many different restaurants, although he'd been at his current restaurant for almost three years.

'Have you ever thought about opening up your own restaurant?' I asked, genuinely intrigued.

His face lit up with the fact that I asked.

'Actually, I've always wanted to open my own restaurant, ideally an Italian restaurant that caters to a healthier crowd as well as those who aren't afraid to indulge and treat themselves. It's very difficult to have both options on the menu though. We were actually thinking about doing it this year, but something came up.' Surprisingly, he didn't seem as disappointed as I imagined he would sound.

Nathaniel became concerned with what Stefan said, 'Stefan, I thought things were starting to smooth out with the planning. What happened?'

There was a moment of silence that was starting to reach a weird level of awkwardness, as if everyone was waiting for someone to say something.

'Ah well, we began to estimate the costs that would be involved. At first, we weren't too sure what everything would add up to, but once we started to calculate all the different expenses and thoroughly reviewed the forecasts, we thought it might be just a little too risky at this moment.' Stefan explained.

'Stefan, if you need help with some of the expenses, I can help you out, or if you need more money, you could consider an investor.' Nathaniel passionately suggested, trying to keep Stefan's hopes up. But it didn't seem like Stefan was out of hope to begin with. I insisted that I could also write an article about the restaurant once it opened or even beforehand to help bring the word out which he very much appreciated.

Somewhere during the discussion, Nathaniel's younger brother left, and it was just us four sitting at the table. I felt bad that I didn't really have the chance to connect and talk much with him.

'Nathaniel...' his mother stopped him. 'The money isn't that big of an issue; we will hopefully be able to still open in a few years' time. It's not like we've found a space to rent or anything and there are still so many things that need to be discussed and finalised. It's not such a simple process, it would need a lot of attention. We need to give this baby a couple more years to fester because... well we've got another baby on the way!' Marissa announced while rubbing her belly. Her pregnancy was barely showing and if she hadn't said anything I would never had noticed. Nathaniel was still focusing on restaurant and didn't realise what his mother was saying.

'Did Victoria already tell you?' Nathaniel asked, he was very confused. He didn't understand what was happening until he saw his mother rubbing her belly and saw me get up to congratulate her.

'Congratulations Mrs Williams! I never would have known. Congratulations to you too Mr Williams!' Marissa seemed a little disappointed in her son's reaction. I don't think she knew why he was confused.

Once Nathaniel had let it sink in, his face lit up.

'Congratulations Mum! This is so exciting! This is why the restaurant is on pause? What wonderful news!' Nathaniel got up to kiss and hug Marissa and Stefan and you could see the happiness and love exude onto each other. Nathaniel looked around for his brother and then got worried because he wasn't there. He started to worry about the health precautions of having a baby at her age, he knew his mum was young when she had him, but still he never expected her to have another child, especially at her age. Regardless, if she and Stefan were happy and willing then so be it. It then sunk in that Nathaniel would have a child the same age as his little brother.

'Where is Mitchel? How did he take the news? Mum, not to sound rude, but I'm surprised you're still able to have a baby.'

'To be honest, so was I, we didn't plan for it but when I found out, I took it as a strange blessing. All my kids have been wonderful so far, why not add another blessing into the family. Mitchel is fine, he's excited but he's just had a lot to do for school. I had a talk with him, as did Stefan. He thought it was weird at first, but then he was fine with it and now he's excited, he can't wait to be a big brother.' Mrs Williams sounded relieved and thankful.

We asked a bunch of questions. Apparently, Marissa and Stefan had been trying to have a baby for a few months now. Mrs Williams was just about five months pregnant and she planned to find out the gender of the baby soon, however Stefan was still deciding whether he wanted to keep it as a surprise. You could see how happy both Marissa and Stefan were that they were going to be having a baby. This would be Stefan's first child even though he'd always considered Nathaniel and Mitchel as his own.

We settled down not long after discussing the pregnancy and talking about it all. Then we had some ice-cream for dessert and Mitchel came back out to sit with us for a little bit. I tried to strike up a conversation with him, so I asked about school and he wasn't very enthusiastic about it. I never used to talk about school either to be honest, so I didn't blame him. It was always such an empty question when someone you didn't really know asked you about it, so I tried a different topic. I asked if he played any video games. I assumed he either went to his room to do that or to read and study. Turns out he plays quite a lot of games, unlike his brother Nathaniel. His favourite games weren't the same as mine, but I've played some of the games that he mentioned.

He led me to his room while Nathaniel continued talking at the table and showed me his games. He was more of a console gamer which is what I was used to. I missed how much time I used to spend playing video games. I didn't think I'd ever have the time to do that anymore, not for too long anyway.

Mitchel stayed in his room playing while I went back out into the dining room. They were all smiling and talking while Nathaniel kept repeating, 'No, I'm not!' I sat back down and asked what I missed. Mrs Williams laughed out loud.

'Oh nothing,' she said. 'We just found out that Nathaniel is dating an older version of his brother.' The soon-to-be-parents again laughed louder.

'No, I'm not!' Nathaniel once again repeated. I couldn't help but blush, from embarrassment or laughter I wasn't sure, but I was blushing.

After some more talking and bantering, something had come to Mrs Williams' mind whilst a look of confusion flashed across her face.

'Nathaniel, before when I told you about the baby, you asked me if Victoria had told me something, has something happened?'

My heart sunk a little. I had thought the coast was clear. No attention was paid to when Nathaniel first brought it up. His face had gone pale from shock. I don't think he knew what to say other than the truth.

He turned his head to face me, almost as if to ask for my permission, but I knew he was going to tell his mother regardless, so I nodded to him and smiled. Nathaniel started by informing Marissa and Stefan about Victoria's condition. They were very upset and distraught to hear about the cancer, but Nathaniel comforted them with the relief that the cancer was detected at an early stage and that it should be able to be treated. Nathaniel then continued by filling them in on the fact that Victoria was pregnant. Marissa seemed a little confused with the news.

'Oh wow! How exciting! That must be difficult to deal with while she's going through cancer treatment at the same time. I always thought that Victoria didn't want to have kids. I remember talking to her about it one time when we had her over for dinner.'

'She doesn't.' Nathaniel stated, 'neither does her husband.'

Marissa's confusion seemed to have increased, then there was a sliver of worry.

'Does that mean they're going to terminate the baby?'

'Not quite Mum, they had another idea in mind.' Nathaniel said bluntly.

'They want to give it up for adoption?'

Nathaniel hesitated a bit, 'Yeah, sort of. They already know the couple whom they're giving the baby to.'

Marissa's face lit up, 'Oh wow, that's so kind of them both, she's such a beautiful woman. I hope that everything goes smoothly. The last thing she needs is more stress and strain on herself. That couple must be feeling extremely happy and grateful.'

Nathaniel sat in front of his mother and stared for what felt like an eternity. He turned his face towards me once again, smiled at me, then looked back at his mother. His body was frozen for a moment, hesitation was taking over again, and his mouth was clenched shut. Nathaniel eventually developed the courage.

'Yes, we are extremely happy and grateful.,' he said.

Stefan smiled from across the table, but Marissa had her eyes moving between myself and Nathaniel with a look of shock and confusion on her face.

'Wait, you mean?' Then it seemed to all click and Marissa's face ignited with surprise whilst her jaw dropped, and she was left fluttering and screaming in both awe and celebration. After the initial shock and excitement, Mrs Williams started to go through everything. I mean, she'd only just met me, only to find out that we were already going to be raising a child together.

'How do you know that you guys will last? Have you any idea how difficult it is to raise a child? Not to mention that you guys are a new couple. The amount of stress and pressure that is going to test your relationship, with or without a newborn! Have you guys even created an environment for a baby to be raised into? We hardly even know you Jacob and this is a seriously large commitment.'

'Mum, we can't really foresee whether our relationship is going to last. Either way, we've already had a number of serious talks about the situation. We both understand the seriousness of raising a baby and how it's going to impact on our lives, and the sacrifices we are going to have to make. Jacob and I both know it's not going to be the easiest thing in the world, but we also know this a once in a lifetime opportunity. I decided to accept this offer, with or without Jacob, and Jacob is graceful enough to want to do this with me. We both want children, and this is an opportunity that does not come along often.' Nathaniel was getting a little defensive but there was no reason, I knew exactly where his Mum was coming from. She knew exactly what it took to raise a child. It just made me wonder how my Mum will react. I could feel the chills run up along my spine.

Nathaniel and I stayed at the table for quite some time. We were answering a number of questions from both Stefan and Marissa, although most were from

Marissa. A lot of them were the same questions that Nathaniel and I asked each other and worked through.

Mrs Williams asked what our plans were if we broke up, if we were prepared. She asked about Victoria's health, but we went through them all and answered each of her questions. We obviously, even though we had dived right in, had discussed all the possibilities. However, I guessed it was important that both mine and Nathaniel's mothers understood that. It would help ease their minds as well as show that Nathaniel and I were taking this seriously. It was only a matter of time now before we told my parents.

Once we got through those questions, we worked through more of what needed to be done before the baby arrived. Our living situation was one thing, but we still needed to decide whether Nathaniel would just move in with me or if we would look for a new place. Then we had to prepare the apartment or potential new place for when the baby arrived; baby-proofing the apartment, creating the nursery, and sourcing all the clothes and equipment we would need. That still depended on whether Nathaniel moved in.

The good news was that Mrs Williams would be having her baby right before us, so we'd be able to have a very helpful guide. I didn't even realise how weird it would be for Nathaniel. He was going to have his new sibling be about a couple of months older than his child. I guess it's only one of the many differences in our situation.

Nathaniel and his mother were getting deep into conversation about babies and all the excitement she felt throughout Nathaniel's early life. It was touching and heart-warming to listen to all of the different moments and memories about Nathaniel. It made me my heart melt to listen to Marissa talk about her son like that. I was starting to get emotional listening to them talk. It was making me thrilled and excited to be raising this child. Stefan had left the conversation and the table moments before, so, I thought I would let Nathaniel and his mother share a moment with each other. I went to see what Mitchel was doing.

I knocked on his door and he let me in. Mitchel was playing a video game. I asked if it was Okay if I sat and watched him play. He said yes and so I did. He started talking to me about the game and how much he enjoys playing adventure games. He reminded me so much of myself. It was very interesting and a little unnerving. I wasn't really sure how to connect with him. I was too angsty at his age to want to actually talk to people.

'I heard about what you told Mum, that you and Nathaniel are going to have a baby. Congratulations!' Mitchel smiled at me. He seemed very open-minded. 'Oh, thank you Mitchel, you're going to be a big brother and an uncle! Hopefully it won't be too much of a change for you.' That would be too stressful for most people.

Mitchel let his excitement radiate on his face.

'I can't wait to be a big brother, but I don't really know how to be an uncle. I'll try my best though.' He sounded sincere, then he asked a question.

'Jacob, if you are having a baby with my brother, does that mean that you love him?'

I was a little taken aback by the question, not that I didn't love Nathaniel, I just had never really told him that, and I wasn't sure if Nathaniel felt the same way.

'Yes, although it may be a bit too early to tell, I think that I do love him.'

'Why? How do you know that you love him?' I couldn't really figure out what Mitchel was trying to get at. I also didn't entirely know how to answer that question, but I tried with as much honesty as I could.

'I feel really good when I'm with him, I care a lot about him, and I think about him almost throughout my entire day. Even though we haven't been together for too long, it's hard to imagine what it would be like not to have him in my life, and I hate thinking that there might be a day where that happens. I think that's how I know that I love him, because I want to protect him from bad things, bad people, and help him when he needs it.' I think I sounded really defensive, but I don't think that Mitchel was coming from an angle of attack. He wanted to learn something; I could tell by the look on his face. He was trying to decipher something himself.

'Have you got a crush on somebody at school?'

Mitchel's face went red and his eyes were bulging out a little bit. He looked at me with a shocked expression, eyebrows up.

'How did you know?' he asked.

I spoke to Mitchel about this crush. I thought it was cute that he was getting all worked up about it. He was only 15 years old, but he wouldn't be the first 15-year-old to have a crush, let alone a girlfriend.

Apparently, Mitchel's friends had heard that his crush also liked him, but he doesn't know what to do. I told him it sounded like the hard part was over considering that he already knew how she felt.

'Maybe you should ask her to go and see a movie or something like that!' It seemed to spark some sort of idea and encouragement in his mind.

After talking with Mitchel, I went back out to sit with Nathaniel and his mother. Stefan was planted in front of the television while Nathaniel and Marissa were still at the table. I really felt for Mitchel. Thinking about the way he was now made think about how I was at that age and how worried I was about liking another boy. Maybe Nathaniel really was dating his brother.

I chuckled as I made my way to the dining table to join them and somehow, they were still talking about how excited they were for both kids to get along. We stayed talking throughout the night until it started to get later than we realised, and we made our way back to the apartment. Nathaniel deciding to come back home with me.

CHAPTER 12

First Trimester

As the weeks went by, it was getting closer to the end Victoria's first trimester. We were checking in with her constantly, to see how she was going and to be with her for anything and everything that she needed. She invited Nathaniel and I to come to the ultrasound during the weekend for the first big milestone. We were thrilled. We promised to take her out for lunch after the appointment. It was the least we could do, as we would forever be in debt to Victoria no matter what we try to do.

A lot had changed in the past few weeks, since meeting Nathaniel's parents. Firstly, I spoke to my parents about Victoria, the baby and Nathaniel. I went alone because I thought it would be the best way to explain everything to my parents. I also didn't want Nathaniel to have to deal with the questions and noise level. When I first told them everything, about Nathaniel's relationship with Victoria, Victoria's situation with cancer and the fact that she was pregnant, they were quite confused, sympathetic, but still confused.

Then I joined the dots for them, I told them that Victoria and her husband didn't want children, but that she wanted to go through with the pregnancy to prove that she could, and to give Nathaniel and I the opportunity of a lifetime. My mum was extremely shocked at first, and then she started questioning everything, saying that I hadn't been with Nathaniel for that long.

I told her everything that Nathaniel had told his mother, and while it took almost the entire night to get through it all, Mum eventually had her mind at ease. She was worried about what might happen in the end, but she was also extremely excited to be having a grandchild. Dad didn't speak too much about it. He was very supportive while taking the time to listen to all the questions. Zach was tremendously excited about the news. He couldn't wait to be an uncle. I knew he'd always wanted a younger sibling, but this was as close as it was going to get.

After I dealt with my parents, I notified work about the entire situation and they were exceptionally comfortable with everything. They had a promotion in line for me and even after I told them about the baby coming, they were still supportive and were continuing to offer me the position. It turned out they had been organising it since before the accident but of course it had to wait until I recovered.

I basically still had the same role but do more admin and data collection work. Nathaniel had been trying something new at work too, to be a lead nurse on the floor. He was also picking up shifts for extra money. He was saving more money because he now lived with me and he didn't have to pay rent. It was the most logical solution and it meant we could get to know each other as much as possible.

That was another thing that happened. Nathaniel moved out of his apartment and into mine. It was only a matter of time before it was going to happen so we thought we might as well jump right in. It would help us test the relationship so that we could be ready before the baby came. It made it easier for us to discuss things and be together while also working to save as much money for the baby as we could. It had been about two weeks now and the adjustment to having someone else constantly living in the house was a strange experience.

I had to make some room to allow Nathaniel to move some of his things into the apartment. It took a moment, but I thought we were starting to develop our flow with one another. We still hadn't had any major arguments, except a few minor clashes, if one of us spent too long in the shower and little things like that. But I was glad he let me know when I was doing something that bothered him. Having him always sleep next to me was definitely the most satisfying part of it all. I got to have his warm body all to myself and I didn't want it any other way.

He was also aware when he might be doing something that got on my nerves and that was Okay. We were still working through the early stages. We were falling in love with each other and then before we knew it, we both fell. We had a better chance of making this work if we were more comfortable with each other, so I was glad that we were compromising when it was necessary. It was funny to think that it had only been four months since we met. Everything has been progressing so fast it feels like it's been a lot longer.

We still had a lot to work on between us, that just comes with being in a relationship, but also a lot had been thrown at us. It sometimes felt like our relationship was on fast forward because we had a time limit of when the baby arrives.

However, it seemed like nothing in comparison to what Victoria was going through and we would be crazy not to do this for ourselves as well as for Victoria. I wish I could just pull out the baby and carry it in me to relieve her of the burden, but unfortunately my anatomy doesn't allow me to do that. Maybe this was a bad idea, I thought, to have Victoria go through this while trying to fight cancer. It was heartbreaking to watch someone else struggle and go through pain, and it feels even worse when part of that pain is because of you and you can't do anything to help them. On top of that, Victoria is the type of person who would never show you if she was in any pain.

Tonight, Nathaniel and I were just having dinner at home. We've been saving as much money as we could. We were tracking quite well; we tried to budget every week and we went out only once or twice a week. It was hard to spend a lot of time with him with our schedules at the moment and I could tell that he got bored sometimes when we don't do anything exciting. I cooked up a lasagne so it would be ready when Nathaniel got home but he was a little bit late. At least that gave the lasagne some time to set.

It was only about ten minutes later that Nathaniel came home from work. He opened the door and looked exhausted. He was visibly in an uneasy mood. I hugged and kissed him when I saw him. He took a minute to get himself ready and then came into the lounge room to eat. I was getting worried that he was starting to burn out from work. He caught me gazing at him and he raised his eyebrow at me and had a smirk on his face.

'What's wrong? Why are you staring at me like that?'

'You just seem stressed out, is everything Okay at work?' I didn't want to upset him or anything, but I just wanted him to be all right.

'Yeah, work is Okay, there was just a sad passing that happened today. There was a young teenager that got into an accident and she had come in, but she was in very critical condition. She was a passenger in her family's car, and they got side swiped. The doctors took her to the ICU and tried their best, but they couldn't do anything. It was hard to see it all and to see her family break down. I've seen these things and have had to deal with them before. As cryptic as it sounds, you have to desensitise yourself to it, which I honestly have, but every now and again you have a situation or a patient that just stays with you. I'll be fine though.'

I was speechless. I didn't know what to say to make him feel better, so, I said nothing. Instead, I got up, filled up a glass of water for Nathaniel and gave him a big hug, because sometimes actions speak louder than words. Nathaniel seemed a tad surprised, but when he hugged back it was evident that he was thankful for the comfort.

After finishing dinner, we spent the night together at home again. That was always my favourite way to spend time with Nathaniel. Cuddling up on the couch and watching movies was something we'd be taking for granted soon enough.

Nathaniel shook me awake, telling me we had to get ready for the ultrasound. I quickly had a shower and we made our way straight to the clinic. Victoria was making her own way there with her husband Greg. Nathaniel was very excited on the way there, but he also seemed to be anxious.

When we arrived at the clinic, Victoria and Greg were already there waiting for us. They said they had only been waiting for a few minutes. All four of us gathered and greeted each other. We entered the clinic and we only had to wait for a couple of minutes before Victoria's name was called to attend a room.

The technician seemed to be confused as to why there were four people entering her room, but then she saw Victoria and it seemed as though she remembered; Victoria must have previously informed her. The technician allowed Victoria to get ready and then started putting the silicone onto Victoria's belly. I was watching Greg's reaction to the ultrasound because I wanted to see if he was regretting this situation, but he didn't seem too interested in the ultrasound. I guess he really didn't want kids. His eyes were averted from the screen and from his wife.

Nathaniel, on the other hand, was extremely excited and wouldn't let go of Victoria's hand.

'The baby seems to be doing well and looks very happy.' The technician informed us all, igniting a spark of joy in us. I don't know how a foetus could look happy, but we went with it. This prompted Greg to sit next to his wife. Greg seemed more worried about Victoria than anything else, asking if she needed anything, and if she was in any pain.

I nudged at Nathaniel to give them some space, but he didn't quite understand what I was saying, so, I asked if they wanted us to give them some space. Greg waited for his wife's answer and when she said it was fine, Greg welcomed us both to stay in the room. He was a very difficult person to read. There was something he was hiding; I just didn't know what it was.

I excused myself from the room to go to the bathroom, but my bladder wasn't the issue, and neither was my stomach. I just needed to wash my face, to clear my head. A lot was running through my mind. I just kept thinking how quickly everything had changed, that I'm soon going to be raising a baby with this guy that I've only been with for a few months. I didn't even know if I was capable of raising a child, and I wasn't sure about anything right now.

I could feel the emotions taking over me. I was feeling extremely overwhelmed and before I knew it the tears started to roll down my face, mixed with the cold refreshing water of the tap. Thankfully, there was nobody else in the bathroom to stop me from letting the tears flow, so I let it all out because that usually helped me get through things eventually. I wasn't too sure why I was crying. I wasn't regretting anything, and I wasn't upset with my life. I think I was just overwhelmed and anxious about what was to come.

I must have been in the bathroom for a while because as soon as I was about to clean myself up, Nathaniel walked in to check on me. His face was confused when he first saw mine, but that quickly became a worried look when he realised that I had been crying. He ran over to me and asked what was wrong before consoling me with his warm and reassuring arms. It took me a second to speak because I didn't really know what to say, and his grip just made me want to cry in his arms. Instead, I slowly spoke about how I was feeling.

I was fine, and I didn't want him to worry about me or anything, it was just that I suddenly became confronted with everything that was happening.

Nathaniel stood in front of me and looked me in the eye.

'Promise me that you're all good?'

'I promise.' I meant it too.

'Do you want to cancel lunch?' Nathaniel said in a serious tone.

'No! Of course not!' That was the absolute least that we could do for both Victoria and Greg, there was no way I was going to cancel lunch over a moment of emotion.

So, we all ended up at a beautiful café not too far from the hospital. It was a cute setup with a rustic style, designed to be a hipster location. We sat outside because the sun was glistening, and it was exceptionally warm. Victoria and Greg were very cosy with each other which was beautiful to see.

We all had a filling lunch and we even had room to order dessert after letting the food settle. Once the dessert had arrived though, something set Victoria off and she ran to the bathroom. I think maybe it was morning sickness, or maybe there was a reaction to the cancer, I wasn't sure. We all got up to check on her, but Greg said he would handle it.

Not long after they both came back to sit down, and they seemed to be Okay. Victoria looked fine, her eyes were red, but she wasn't shaken up or anything like that. I felt bad though, we were doing this to her. I could tell she was putting on a brave face, it was the same thing that I would do in the situation.

'Is everything Okay?' I asked. I was getting more worried as time went on.

'Everything is fine, it was just the chocolate. I think the strong scent just got to me.' She smiled, but it didn't stop her from eating the dessert anyway.

We tried to ask her about how her treatment was going, she said it was tough. Greg stared at me after that.

It seemed like it was a glare of resentment, but I wasn't too sure. He must really despise us at this moment and I honestly didn't blame him.

I kind of hated us too right now, I hated watching this happen to Victoria. I really wanted to know what Greg was truly thinking about this entire situation. I still didn't really know too much about him. Maybe I could speak to Nathaniel about it.

'There was another thing I wanted to ask you both.' Victoria continued. 'I know we briefly spoke about it earlier, but in a few more weeks we will be able to learn the gender of the baby. Have you guys thought about whether you'd like to know the gender?'

Nathaniel and I had discussed it, although we didn't agree on a conclusion. Nathaniel really wanted to know beforehand, so that he could plan the nursery and prepare clothes and blankets. I, on the other hand, wanted the surprise. I supposed it was more than plausible for Nathaniel to know whilst I still got a surprise. It might be difficult, but it could work as long as he doesn't blurt it out. I doubted though that Nathaniel would be able to keep a secret from me, and it might cause some tension.

'We're still deciding,' Nathaniel responded. 'Jacob wants to keep it a surprise, but I can't wait to find out!'

We spent the rest of lunch going over whether or not we should find out, then we went over baby names, for both girls and boys. Even Greg was getting involved and throwing some names out on the table. It's safe to say that even with four of us discussing and suggesting names, we still never came to a consensus. Thankfully, we still had some time before that day comes.

CHAPTER 13

Burning Out

It had been a couple of weeks since reaching the first trimester milestone, and it was almost time to find the out the gender of the baby. I decided I still wanted to keep it as a surprise and Nathaniel was going to find out with Victoria. I felt like I'd barely gotten to see Nathaniel recently. I was having dinner alone again and he wouldn't be home for another hour at least. I kept cooking for him, but he was never home when I ate so it was tough. It was difficult because we were both working overtime to try and save as much as we could, which we were still doing quite well with. I just hated how distant it all felt. We leapt into things extremely fast and we barely had time to enjoy each other in the early stages before going full speed ahead. It was also the first time since the accident that my legs were beginning to ache. I needed to rest them and let them breathe. My body was readjusting to being back at work full time.

Nathaniel finally got home, and he sounded exhausted. He heated up some food and came to sit next to me as he ate. He was telling me that he wished he could be the one to cook for me more but hates that he's always home late. We were discussing a few things about our budget and about work. We evaluated that after about a month, we could slow down and he could take less shifts.

Nathaniel always clung to me when he got back from the hospital. Ever since he caught me in the bathroom after the ultrasound, Nathaniel has been cautious with me. I spoke to him about it because I noticed he was a little on edge. He was worried that he was going to lose me. He thought that because of everything that happened I'd get too overwhelmed and would leave.

I thought that Nathaniel felt somewhat responsible for everything that we're going through. He told me one night that he hoped he never has to raise the baby alone. I hope he doesn't have to either. I knew deep in my heart that I wouldn't leave, and I think Nathaniel knew that too, but he was a lot more affectionate lately, which I must admit felt good.

We had both been working ourselves crazy, living on a low budget and trying to enjoy every minute that we could spend together. We'd had such busy schedules lately, but we decided to organise a dinner this weekend, so we could unwind a little bit and catch a break. For now, Nathaniel and I stayed home again, watched a movie, and cuddled, until the cuddling led to something a little more.

It felt amazing, it was passionate and fulfilling. It was strange to think how comfortable I'd gotten with sex. I instantly wanted to go for another round. It made me think about how much I love Nathaniel. It made me think that sex sometimes does build a connection and can show a love that we couldn't always communicate with words. We lay together in bed after we finished and talked to each other until we fell asleep.

After an intense week, both for Nathaniel and me, we were getting dressed up to go on our fancy dinner date. It was refreshing to get dressed up and this was one of the first times that I got to see Nathaniel dress up. I must say he looked superbly stunning. Nathaniel decided that he was going to drive and honestly, I was glad because it meant that I could be a passenger and admire him without any distractions. I noticed that he looked happy and seeing him smile and be joyful made me feel that happiness too.

Nathaniel turned to me mid drive and noticed that I had my eyes set on him.

'Why are you staring at me like that?'

'I'm just glad that we are trying to spend time together outside of the house. Also, because I love you. Plus, you look hot!' I said, counting the reasons with my fingers. I wanted to make him feel good.

I saw his smile grow and his cheekbones tighten.

'I love you too.' Nathaniel said through his grin.

When we stopped at the traffic lights, he turned my head and gave me a kiss. It made me feel all hot and bothered, but then the lights turned green again before I could do anything too frisky.

When we got to the restaurant, Nathaniel locked my door when I tried to reach for the handle so that he could walk around and open it for me. Just like last time, I'm not injured anymore though. Nathaniel can be cheesy and chivalrous when he wants to be, and I couldn't complain. I thought it was cute. I froze instantly as Nathaniel escorted me out of the car. The air was icy and made my hair rise.

Thankfully, when we stepped into the restaurant, the warmth welcomed us immediately. The lights were very romantic, dimmed to a very comfortable level. Almost directly after entering the restaurant, a waiter arrived, greeted us, and ushered us to a table. The restaurant was elegantly designed and even though it was filled with people it surprisingly wasn't too loud. Taking in the atmosphere, I noticed there were a lot of couples, laughing and enjoying each other's company while they ate.

We sat down together and while I was continuing to admire the atmosphere of the restaurant Nathaniel looked at me, smirking and snickering. He kept staring so I questioned him.

'Why are you laughing at me?'

'You just look beautiful, and I'm glad that we are doing this.' Nathaniel gazed into my eyes as he spoke. 'I know it's been tough the past few weeks, maybe even months. We jumped very far really quickly, and I know it will be worth it when the baby arrives, I've just been missing you a little more recently. Even though we live together, work has been getting in the way a fair amount. It's just a temporary stretch that we have to go through before we get to our goal, but we are almost there, and we can slow down our schedules soon. I'm just so glad and excited that I get to go through this journey with you Jacob. I love you so much and you make me feel genuinely happy and honoured.'

I could feel my face start to ache because I was smiling uncontrollably. I felt so flattered in this moment, and I absolutely adored that he vocalised his thoughts even though we were in public. I honestly had to fight to hold back the tears. My night was already made, and it had only just begun. I grabbed his hands and held them.

'I love you too Nathaniel. I know our lives have changed so much but I'm excited that mine is moulding in a way to fit with you and me together.'

We smiled, looking into each other's eyes while our hands were held. All of the surroundings that I was previously absorbing shifted into a complete blur as my eyes heavily focused onto Nathaniel's. It took us a second before we broke off and opened our menus, but not before we shared a kiss. I was still trying to adjust to the PDA.

'Now let's eat.' He suggested. We were quick in choosing what to order for food, and of course, we kept a menu on the side for dessert afterwards.

We talked quite a lot while waiting for our food. Nathaniel was talking about work and he said that Victoria had finally dropped shifts to three days a week. She had a couple more weeks before she wanted to cut back completely because she had already taken time off at the beginning of her treatment. Greg and Nathaniel had been telling her for ages to at least cut down on the amount of work she does. She was a little stubborn sometimes and she certainly didn't let other people make decisions for her.

Nathaniel mentioned that he couldn't wait to slow down from his work so that we could spend more time with each other. Before the food came, I asked Nathaniel how his Mum was going with her pregnancy. Thankfully, everything was good, there were no complications so far and hopefully there wouldn't be any.

The food was delicious and so was the date accompanying me. I would catch myself staring at Nathaniel, talking to my subconscious about how lucky and grateful I was to be with him and for everything that was happening. Nathaniel was browsing the dessert menu and asking what I felt like eating, but I wasn't paying attention and I only realised it when he started waving his hands in front of my face.

'Hello?!' he said as he waved, 'Earth to Jacob, why are you staring into my soul like that?'

'Am I not allowed to admire the view?' I smirked as I was forced back into reality. Nathaniel chuckled at my response.

'Could you pick a dessert please, babe?' Nathaniel pushed.

I told him to surprise me with something, I'm not too picky, especially when it comes to desserts. Before I knew it, the waiter arrived with a sensational chocolate fudge brownie with ice-cream and strawberries for Nathaniel and me to share. Luckily, we have the same taste when it comes to dessert. He let me take the first bite and when the spoon cut through the brownie, a warm chocolate sauce oozed out. Mixed with the ice-cream and strawberry it tasted absolutely mouth-watering, like something created by a divine being.

It wasn't too long before the dessert was finished, but we were in the midst of a food coma, or at least I was, and had no intention of moving anytime soon. We sat there for many moments in silence, his mind was elsewhere, and I was pretty sure I knew what he was thinking.

'Are you excited about tomorrow?' I asked. Tomorrow was the day that he was going with Victoria to find out the gender of the baby, 'Yeah, I really am.' He didn't even have to ask what I was talking about because he knew exactly what I meant. We were on the same page, but not entirely. 'Are you sure you don't want to change your mind about coming? I wish we could do this together.' It was obvious that he wanted me to do this with him, for me to go and find out with him and make it all cute and romantic, but something in my mind kept stopping me, my heart was telling me to keep it a surprise. Everything had just happened so fast that I wanted this surprise to make it feel like this wasn't all so logistical.

'I'm sure, I'm sorry. I don't want you to get upset with me, I just have a feeling that I should keep it as a surprise.' I did feel a little guilty in a sense, because I was saying no to a lifelong memory, but at the same time I was saying yes to another one.

'I would never!' Nathaniel said, then he leaned over the table pouting his lips, asking for a kiss. I met his lips with mine for a quick peck and then flashed my smile for him. I was humbled that he was able to respect my decision and not try too hard to persuade me. We finished our drinks and made our way home after paying for our meals, Nathaniel took the bill this time around.

When we finally got home, we went straight to the bedroom and we didn't even bother to put on a movie. We lay in the bed and Nathaniel was way too excited about tomorrow to sleep. His hands were starting to get a little frisky. He continued, caressing my body and kissing my neck before his lips found their way to mine. We were going at it with each other and it wasn't long before we were both naked, letting our bodies do the talking. The passion and desire were exuding from our bodies as we pressed ourselves into each other, moaning and making love throughout the night, our bodies heating up and dirtying the sheets.

By the time I woke up, Nathaniel was gone. The sun sneaked in through the curtains and onto my face. When I turned to face the other way, my hands searched for his body, but they were only met with bed sheets. The empty bed made me realise he had already left for the ultrasound. It was ten in the morning and my stomach refused to let me sleep in any longer. I stripped the bed and put the sheets in the washing machine, then I went to the bathroom to have a shower. I could tell from the fogged mirror that Nathaniel had done the same thing not too long ago. We both enjoyed having hot, steamy showers. Right now, that and food were the only two things I needed this morning.

After the shower, I made myself some breakfast to help tame the beast within my belly. I was going to make some for Nathaniel too, but I didn't know when he would be coming home. I assumed he would be a tad later, so I ate alone and read a book for a while. Only about half an hour after I began reading, Nathaniel walked through the door. I wondered why he and Victoria hadn't gone out for lunch.

The moment we locked eyes Nathaniel's smile grew immensely. He ran over to me and threw the book out of my hand, replacing my grip on the book with his hands. He pulled me up and kissed me ever so gently through his overbearing smile. It lasted longer than necessary, but I wasn't complaining. His happiness helped light up the entire apartment. When he withdrew from the kiss, he threw his arms around me, squeezing himself into me. He forced me back onto the couch and we lay there for a while, cuddling each other and admiring each other's touch.

After laying for a moment, Nathaniel brought his head back and yelled 'We are having a boy!'

My eyes almost popped entirely out of my eyes.

'Nathaniel!' I yelled back at him, 'What the hell?!' I didn't know how to feel, I was angry at him but also excited about the news.

Seconds later, Nathaniel started giggling loudly and then cracked into a laugh. He tried to speak through the cackling, 'I'm only joking, it's a girl! No, wait. I think it's…' He continued to laugh while I frowned at him; this was not a very fun game. Before I could open my mouth and say anything he continued, 'I'm sorry babe, I love you so much, I'm just in a really good mood, I saw the opportunity and I took it.' He always knew the right thing to say, even if he was being a tease.

'I love you too.' I said, kissing him on the cheek reluctantly while I withheld my anger, I could never stay angry at Nathaniel. He always did something that made me smile.

CHAPTER 14

Exchange for a Miracle

Nathaniel was in an energetic mood all day after learning about the baby's gender. He was always excited but after the ultrasound this morning, he was on a buzz that was bigger than usual. We were about to go over to Victoria's place for dinner. We were getting takeout, so she didn't have to cook because Greg had a work meeting tonight. We ordered pizza and we picked it up on our way to Victoria's house. She was craving cheese pizza and garlic bread and I could never say no to pizza.

The food was still warm in our hands when we arrived at Victoria's. Her face lit up once she opened the door, I wasn't sure if it was because she was happy to see us or because the smell of the pizza was invading her nostrils. She was in a beautiful, comfortable looking dress that still allowed her cute, protruding belly to be outlined. We went inside and we all sat together at the table. Victoria was happy to have company, pizza and garlic bread and we didn't want her to spend Saturday night alone.

When we stepped into the house, I was immediately welcomed by the vibrant colours that filled it. The lounge room had a beautiful light caramel coloured paint that matched with the furniture and the rest of the house. There were so many paintings and artworks that decorated the house. My favourite was an extremely daring painting of a tiger that was laying down in an elegant pouncing position while glaring directly at you.

The house was very inviting, as was Victoria. We sat at the table, eating pizza while the television was on in the background. I asked Victoria about the paintings because I was intrigued. She claimed that they were Greg's touch to the house's interior. He enjoyed dressing up the house with different types of décor and Victoria approved of it all. It made me think of Greg in a different way. Now that I thought about it, I didn't know Greg all too well, and I needed to fix that soon.

We spoke to Victoria about how she was feeling. She seemed to dodge the question. She said that the treatment had been going well. I tried to ask again.

'But Victoria, how are you feeling? Not just about the treatment, but in general. Is there anything we can help you with?' She made a face as if to say that everything was fine, nonetheless I needed her to know that we were here.

'Yeah, I'm feeling pretty good. Sometimes I feel a little heavy and drained, tired, but other than that I feel all right. In terms of you guys, I mean, there isn't that much more you guys can do for me. It's sweet though that you guys want to. You're both always calling me and checking up on me and feeding me.' She started to choke up a tad, but she never shed a tear. 'I'm honestly grateful for you guys and I'm excited to be doing this for you both. Don't feel like you aren't doing enough because you are.' She smiled at us before filling her mouth with a slice of pizza.

She was still insistent about going to work and not cutting back on her hours too much. I asked her about Greg and how he was coping. He apparently was doing well considering everything. In a quick attempt, we tried to bring up the subject of getting Victoria a gift of some sort as our way to thank her for everything. Previously, Nathaniel had made an effort to discuss it at lunch one time while Greg was there, however, it didn't turn out too well and not an ounce of progress had been made at the lunch or since.

So, we brought up the notion again, but almost as soon as the idea was mentioned, Victoria shut it down. We let it go but we gave it another shot by easing into the conversation. We asked Victoria about what she planned to do after giving birth. Of course, this depended on the state of her cancer, but she was excited to just relax and watch movies at home for a week or two and then jump back into work.

Earlier on, Nathaniel and had I discussed what we thought would be the best gift to give Victoria. There wasn't exactly a card or a staple gift to give someone that says: 'thanks for giving me a child'. We had to brainstorm a little and think what would be best for Victoria. In our minds we had something planned. A fair amount of our overtime work was in order to save to give Victoria some money. She'd refused that offer initially, but it was time that we tried again.

'Victoria,' Nathaniel started. 'Jacob and I were thinking that we definitely need to get you something to say thank you for everything that you are doing.' As soon as he'd finished, I braced myself for Victoria's response.

'No,' Victoria interrupted. 'Nathaniel, I've already spoken to you before about this and you already know that I don't want or need anything. I don't need money, I don't need a new car, I don't need holidays or anything of that sort. Jacob,' she turned her attention and focus to me and took a breath. 'I haven't yet spoken to you personally about it but I'm telling you now, I do not want anything, you have already both been extremely helpful with the situation. You've been on board with everything, keeping me company, taking me out to lunch and staying by my side. In all honesty, that's more than enough for me.'

I thought I would try to bargain with her to see if she would budge at all.

'What about Greg? Wouldn't he appreciate it if we could do something to help out the both of you, and at least help relax you afterwards?'

'No. Thank you for the gesture, I truly am grateful that you guys are willing to do something, but there is nothing that Greg nor I will accept. I would genuinely prefer it if you saved your money for when the baby comes. That way you guys can be prepared if anything happens financially.' Victoria was stern in her answer.

At that moment, I gave up trying to convince Victoria otherwise. Nathaniel had already tried to bring it up in the past a couple of times, now this time neither of us were successful in attempting to persuade Victoria. Maybe we could just surprise her with something small. In the meantime, the three of us continued the night on the lounge, still eating the remnants of pizza that remained. The melting cheese made my tastebuds dance and my stomach sing.

After finishing her last slice of pizza for the time being, Victoria looked towards me and asked why I didn't want to know the gender of the baby. It wasn't probing or rude, it was out of curiosity. I tried to explain to her that the element of surprise somehow made it feel more special and real, but I couldn't quite articulate that, although I wouldn't be upset if I found out the gender prior to the birth. I followed up by asking when she was planning to take time off work completely. She was already almost at the five-month mark.

'I'm just going to ride out the wave and see how I feel,' Victoria responded with no hesitation. 'I don't get too tired usually but of course there are some days when I just want to eat and sleep.' She laughed at the thought. 'In saying that, I think that when I'm further along in the pregnancy, I will definitely have to stop completely at some point, but right now the cut back has been a good balance and it's easy for me to maintain.'

Nathaniel was sitting quietly while Victoria and I continued talking. I could sense that something was bothering him, and I knew him well enough now that I had a pretty solid idea of what the issue was. I thought it would be more appropriate to talk to him about it when we get home, which judging by the clock wouldn't be too much longer. Victoria was starting to get tired and I thought it would be best if we let her sleep. Greg should be home soon anyway. We cleaned up our mess, said goodnight and headed towards the door.

As we stepped out off the front porch, the two brightest headlights in the entire car industry made its way up the driveway. Greg was home.

We quickly said hello and goodbye. Greg thanked us for keeping Victoria company, and then we made our way to the car. I decided to drive home because judging by the number of yawns, Nathaniel was more tired than I was, plus I wanted him to be able to think, or not think, if that's what he needed to do. I didn't talk to him or interrupt him at all in the car. I let him continue to look outside the window, like a little kid lost in his thoughts. I had the music on, but it wasn't very loud, just loud enough for me to enjoy the drive and quiet enough to not interrupt Nathaniel.

When we got to the apartment Nathaniel went straight into the shower, I think he wanted to cleanse his mind. I thought about surprising Nathaniel in the shower, but I didn't think that he would be in the mood. I needed to talk to him, I didn't want his mind to keep festering and I had a feeling that if I had a shower right after him that he would fall asleep straight away. So, instead, I sat on the bed after getting changed and waited for Nathaniel to finish his shower. I could always have mine in the morning or after we spoke.

I was lying in bed by the time Nathaniel actually got out of the shower, it was definitely a little longer than usual. He walked in the bedroom and I saw his white towel wrapped around him, tight around his waist, his butt was still outlined quite clearly. His hair looked to be wet still and there were droplets trickling slowly down his body that made him look beautiful as ever, but as my eyes met his he let out a forced smile before putting on a pair of boxers and joining me in bed.

Nathaniel faced away from me, but I rolled him around and I gave him a kiss and cuddled to try and cheer him up, I was a little nervous because I wasn't entirely sure how he would react. I held onto him a little longer than I usually did. Before I could try any further to coddle him, he looked at me with a cute and confused face.

'Is everything Okay?' he asked.

'Is everything Okay?' I repeated back to Nathaniel. 'You tell me. I already know that something is bothering you and I'm pretty certain I know exactly what it is.' I think I was a bit snappier than I intended to be.

Nathaniel's already weak smile faded to an even less enthusiastic smile. He seemed a tad thrown.

'Is it that obvious?' Nathaniel replied, with a voice of disappointment.

'Only to me.' I tried to continue to comfort him and empathise with him. 'I know that you really wanted to get something for Victoria, that you still do. I could sense the frustration when she kept refusing our offers.'

'It's not only that,' Nathaniel interrupted. 'Victoria kept saying that we were so involved and how helpful we were with her, as if that isn't supposed to be a given or something. I just, I don't feel like we even do that much for her and there's no way that I'm not going to be able to get her a gift.'

'Yeah, I thought so too. We haven't really done anything that's out of the way.' Nathaniel seemed to be passionate about what he wanted and disinterested in whatever I had to say but I was here to agree and support him. 'Nathaniel, listen, you don't have to explain it to me or try to persuade me. I still think that we should get something for Victoria regardless of what she says and if she chooses not to use it or take it then that's fine. I know we spoke about it before and we obviously struggled with great difficulty trying to find out a solution. I have an idea though, one that I'll keep a secret for now, but as for the other, I think we should get them a week away at a nice resort, maybe one that isn't too far away. I know it's not a huge gesture, but it feels like it's a compromise that is still notable and this way, Victoria and Greg can use it when it best suits them. It's something that they can both enjoy. What do you think babe?'

Nathaniel's face lifted as an invisible weight released from his shoulders.

'I think it's perfect. Hopefully Victoria won't get angry at us, but also, too bad if she does.' He kissed me and kept kissing me until he broke off and said, 'Thank you Jacob, I'm so glad that we are on the same page.' He grabbed my neck and pulled me in, continuing to kiss me. When he broke off for air he quickly asked with a curiosity in his voice, 'What is your other idea babe?'

I smirked at Nathaniel and leaned back in for more kisses. He let me have a couple more before he pulled away and repeated his question to me.

'That's for me to know. We can discuss it in the future, but I think it's something that you will agree with me on. Trust me.' I reassured him.

'If you say so.' Nathaniel face expressed not much more than confusion, but I could also sense that he was relieved.

I was glad that we'd had our talk. This time, I took hold of Nathaniel and let myself give in to him, my lips connecting with his while I shifted my body on top of him, running my fingers through his hair and letting them manoeuvre down his body, removing his boxers while he took off mine.

CHAPTER 15

A Different Kind of Shower

It was reaching the end of the second trimester and now that we had organised our gift for Victoria and Greg, it was a lot easier for Nathaniel and me to forecast our budget. We would only need a couple more weeks until we could slow down the hours at work, no more overtime and possibly even less hours than beforehand. We were initially going to take a week off together, but we decided to save it for when the baby arrived.

I'd already spoken to my manager about what was happening. They were tremendously excited for me and they were also very flexible about the situation. They said that when the baby came, they would easily give me time off and even cater to my schedule after that if there were going to be any changes. I was going to be getting six weeks parental leave but if I wanted to take more on annual leave then I could. Nathaniel said that his boss was just as accepting and willing to accommodate to his when the baby was born. In the meantime, the two of us were planning to continue working and saving as much as we could.

Nathaniel had just come back from visiting his Mum. He spent lunch with her to catch up with her, check up on how she was doing. He had something in his hand, it was an envelope, but it was very neatly decorated. He handed it to me and gave me a look that I couldn't quite decipher.

'What is it?' I asked.

'Open it and have a look.' He replied, sounding a little enthusiastic.

I meticulously opened the envelope, not wanting to ruin the delicate design. Inside was a beautiful, intricately crafted invitation, written out to both me and Nathaniel together. My smile widened as I read our names together. The invitation was inscribed for us to attend a baby shower held by Nathaniel's mother. I looked up at him. I questioned why she was throwing one, considering it wasn't her first child, not that there was anything wrong with that, I just assumed she wouldn't be bothered.

Nathaniel reminded me that it was her first kid with Stefan, so she wanted to make it special for him. That was fair. The date for the baby shower was for next Saturday and she invited us to be a part of it even though it might be a little different. I looked back up at Nathaniel after reading the invitation and appreciating the detail, he was giving me the same look that he did earlier.

'Why do you keep looking at me like that?'

'Why do you think?' Nathaniel replied, but I honestly had no clue what he was referring to. I tried to wrap my brain around an answer, but I didn't really understand it.

'Do you think that I wouldn't want to go? I obviously want to go if that's what you're asking.'

Nathaniel smiled.

'Oh, you're definitely coming, silly. We don't have a choice about that, but that wasn't what I was thinking about. I just thought, why don't we do that?'

'Do what?' I asked, knowing exactly what he was about to ask.

'Why don't we throw a baby shower as well? It could be super fun and exciting!' The enthusiasm was oozing from his voice, he sounded like a little kid asking for a new toy, but for some reason I just wasn't getting the same vibe.

'Uh, I mean, wouldn't it be a little weird considering neither of us are actually pregnant? It would also be a little costly too, unless we just do something small?' I didn't mean to shut it down so quickly, I just thought I was being reasonable, but I could visibly see the dissatisfaction and heartbreak cover his face, so I instantly tried to change my tone. 'Why don't you ask Victoria and see what she thinks about it? She might like to do something about it all.'

'Yeah, I suppose that it might be a little strange considering our circumstance, but isn't our entire situation out of the ordinary? I'll obviously see what Victoria thinks, that would be a great idea to get Victoria involved but I doubt that she will want to.' Nathaniel's mood wasn't as positive as I'd hoped, it was clear he was still beaten down about it all.

I felt guilty, maybe I should be excited to throw something like a baby shower, to celebrate everything. I just feel as though it would be awkward and somewhat excruciating.

Nathaniel and I weren't seeing Victoria until the next week. Their schedules at work didn't clash this week but I think considering Nathaniel's excitement, he decided he would try to call her to try get a response. I think he wanted to know so that he could start planning something, it was like his expression was locked within him and he just wanted to be given the key. The phone rang and Nathaniel put it on speaker so that I could also listen, it took a moment before Victoria eventually picked up the phone.

'Hello?' Victoria answered.

'Hey Victoria,' Nathaniel replied, 'how's everything going?' You knew Nathaniel was nervous when he started beating around the bush.

'Everything is good, just about to have lunch with Greg, what about you?'

Nathaniel hesitated to say anything at first. 'If you're busy then I can call later, it's not a problem.'

'No, that's fine, what did you want to talk about?'

Nathaniel explained that his mother had just sent us an invitation for the baby shower and that it planted the idea within his own mind, he also managed to throw me way under the bus by notifying Victoria that I suggested to call her and ask what she thought about the whole thing.

'Umm,' Victoria paused for more than a moment. 'Honestly, I'm not too sure if I'd be up for something like that, I wouldn't really enjoy it so much and it might feel kind of strange if I was there. Wouldn't it make more sense for you guys to do that without me anyway? You are going to be the parents after all.' Victoria sounded both flattered and flat at the same time.

'Yeah, I suppose, I just thought I would see if you wanted any input on it all. Enjoy your lunch!' They bid their goodbyes and Nathaniel hung up the phone.

Once again, I watched the happiness escape from Nathaniel's face. I could almost hear his heart trying not to burst after Victoria's rejection. He slouched on the couch after hanging up the phone, a deep, heavy sigh released from his mouth. I grabbed him, put my arm around him and gave him a big hug, forcing him to lie on the couch while I overpowered his body. He sank his head into my shoulder and then he moved his head back to give me a kiss on the cheek.

'Why don't we compromise babe?' I asked Nathaniel, an idea came into my head and I just wanted to make him happy.

'No, you were right. Victoria didn't want to have a baby shower and I could tell you felt the same way. Plus, I guess it would be wiser to save the money.' The defeated tone of his voice was a little upsetting to listen to.

'Nathaniel, instead of throwing a party as a baby shower, why don't we just have a dinner and invite a bunch of people, we could do it here or even have it at a restaurant. It might still cost a bit, but it would still be cheaper than an entire baby shower.' My words seemed to enlighten his eyes.

Nathaniel sat back up as if that idea had never occurred to him. It was as if he thought only a huge party or no party. He looked as if he was trying to say something, but then he paused for a moment, thinking about something.

'One slight issue Jacob. What about our parents?'

'What about our parents?' I questioned.

'Do we invite both of them?' Nathaniel asked, he had a worried look on his face.

'Yeah, I don't see why not, it could be interesting. It's about time they meet, plus I don't exactly have all too many friends to invite. Maybe we can have our parents arrive earlier so that they can bond and get to know each other beforehand.' The situation sounded a little more plausible in my own head than it did aloud.

Nathaniel seemed a little hesitant at first but then he agreed.

'I guess we can just invite them both and we'll see what happens.'

'So, what you are telling me is that my compromise was a success and that I was able to find a suitable solution? You're welcome!' I winked at Nathaniel, teasing him. 'We can enjoy all the baby games you can think of at your mother's baby shower.'

Saturday came and we were knocking on the door of Nathaniel's mother's house with a bundle of baby clothes wrapped in a beautiful blue package. Nathaniel had initially bought clothes both for a boy and girl but left the girls clothes at home after learning that his mother was having a boy. When the knob of the door twisted and the door swung open, Marissa was at its entrance welcoming us both with a beautiful smile and open arms that allowed us to see her gorgeous bump. We'd arrived early to help set up with the decorations and the food.

Walking into the house, Marissa's belly was a lot more visible up close and it was giving her a shimmery glow. Looking around, the house did seem somewhat decorated already, the food and the snacks for the games were mainly prepared beforehand, and we just needed to set up the tables, balloons, streamers, baby games and a crafts section for baby onesie designs.

There was still roughly an hour and a half left until the guests were to arrive. Stefan and Mitchel were nowhere in sight, Marissa said Mitchel preferred not to be part of the celebrations, Stefan had to work but he'll be home later, and Mitchell was at his friend's house. For the next hour, Nathaniel and I followed Marissa's direct orders and steadily helped finalise the remainder of the set up. Observing the decorations, we added the final additions to the house that made it look like the baby shower was ready to commence. Not too long after, there was knocking at the door and the first wave of the guests arrived.

The baby shower was overall a success. Marissa celebrated her baby with friends and family, and eventually Stefan came home early enough to enjoy some of the party as well. We had fun playing different games and doing different activities. We all made designs on baby onesies and shirts, we wrote down some baby names for suggestions, and blind tasted different flavours of baby food. Some of Marissa's friends put on the adult diapers and had a race on all fours. Once the party was over and the guests had left, Nathaniel and I stayed back to help clean up the mess and reorganise the house back to its original state.

Nathaniel and I made our way home shortly after we helped clean up. My body was starting to ache, and I could feel the exhaustion taking over my body. I wondered if Nathaniel was feeling the same thing. I was definitely quite relieved that we weren't going to be organising another shower for ourselves. There was a lot of planning and setting up involved and that wasn't really my thing. It was fun to participate, and it was heartwarming to see Marissa enjoying herself and being excited about the entire thing. It was evident where Nathaniel got his enthusiasm from.

Nathaniel organised a dinner in two weeks to celebrate our version of a baby shower. There were still some of his friends that I hadn't met, and from my side I was only inviting three of my close friends. They'd only met Nathaniel one time when I had gotten out of the hospital, and Nathaniel had made me tell them to come over. They weren't impressed at the time that I had hidden the accident from them, and they were also quite surprised when they first heard that we were having a baby. First, they were hesitant, but now they were all on board and as supportive as always.

CHAPTER 16

Weekend of a Lifetime

It was Friday night and Nathaniel had just told me that he wasn't going to be home until after 6pm. He was finishing up at work. Victoria was there today, and she had recently hit the seven-month milestone. Nathaniel and I had reached our own milestone of being together officially for six months a couple of weeks back, but with everything going on we hadn't been able to celebrate.

Technically, we celebrated last month with the baby shower and it was a huge success. It was the first time that our parents had met. We had our friends there as well and our parents got along quite well. Both of our brothers were excited to meet one another and apparently, they'd been in contact with each other since and have met up without us. Our parents were bonding with each other also, our mothers more so than our fathers, mainly because my Dad didn't speak too much on first meeting.

There wasn't any visual tension which was good and there was still a lot of conversation. Marissa and Juliet were talking for ages throughout the night, and they've also met up without our presence, as it only made sense that they'd want to get to know each other more considering the speed at which everything has been progressing. Stefan and Anthony had only met once more after the baby shower but according to my Mum, they were meshing together just fine. We supposedly had nothing to worry about.

My friends were excited to be spending more time with not only Nathaniel, but also with me. It was difficult to keep in touch and catch up with them regularly, so it was refreshing to see them. I also met a lot of friends that Nathaniel invited, some from the hospital and some from elsewhere. They all seemed quite nice and were very friendly, with the exception of a few who delivered some cold, judgemental stares. I didn't tell Nathaniel though because I didn't want to cause any drama, but it was possibly because they remembered me from the hospital. Victoria wasn't in the mood to come to the baby shower, so she didn't. I definitely noticed her absence, and most likely Nathaniel did too, however we had our own dinner with her the day afterwards to accommodate the fact.

This weekend was our first weekend without having worked overtime during the week. Nathaniel and I had finished organising our gift for Victoria. We settled on a week-long getaway for both Victoria and Greg at a beautiful resort that wasn't too far away from home. Since we had finalised the gift, we were able to sort out our finances and we were able to cut back from the extra hours. We even had a bit of money to splurge on ourselves, which is exactly what we planned to do this weekend.

We were starting with dinner tonight. I was at home waiting for Nathaniel so we could get ready and go. He should be home from work by around 6:30 and I still had some time, so I decided to have a quick shower. I had a relaxing, boiling hot shower that steamed up the entire bathroom, and it was by no means a 'quick' shower. By the time I got out, Nathaniel was home and now he was the one waiting for me.

'Hey Baby!' I gave Nathaniel a peck, water was still dripping from my chest. 'Sorry, I took a little longer than I thought I would. Are you ready to go?'

Nathaniel looked up at me with a questioning look, the tiredness still in his eyes.

'Yes, of course. I'm ready whenever you are.' I asked if there was a dress code for this dinner. He always had a thing for picking restaurants and not telling me where we were going, mainly because I know a lot of their backgrounds from work.

'Casual will be fine.' I could hear him laughing under his breath.

I got dressed and Nathaniel approved of my outfit. We got into the car and obviously Nathaniel drove. It was so beautiful outside. The sun had set already but it was still warm. The roads were familiar. I thought we were going to a restaurant that we've been to before. He had noticed that I was taking in our surroundings on our drive. Nathaniel asked if I'd figured where we were going, I had. The Italian restaurant near the beach, where we had our first date. The last time I was here I was still on crutches.

Dinner was perfect, not just the food, but the entire experience. The restaurant was still decorated and set up in the same way. Nothing had changed in the time since we last came, nothing except for Nathaniel and me. So much had happened in the half a year since we were last here. This place brought back some nostalgic memories, but they weren't as nostalgic as they were beautiful. The best part about the memories was that we were here again, making new ones, with each other.

We didn't stay for dessert. Instead, we left the restaurant after dinner and went for a walk along the beach, once again getting ice-cream on the way. The weather was starting to cool down. I could see the goosebumps rise on Nathaniel's skin. I took off my jacket and put it over his shoulders.

Before I knew it, we were at the beach and about to walk on the shore, my hand melting into his, until his slipped away. Nathaniel stopped in front of me and then bent down onto one knee. My heart dropped for a split second and then started pounding, but then the weight from my foot released as Nathaniel loosened my shoelace.

'I know you like the feeling of the sand,' he said while his face rose to look at mine, he could probably see the shock on my face, 'What's wrong?'

His question wasn't what I initially thought it would be, but it brought me back to reality. Then I wondered, what would I have said if he did ask, would it have been too soon to say yes? I suppose with that logic, everything else that had happened up to now has also been too soon. I guess it's not always as traditional as it could be when you're in a gay relationship, but then again everyone is different.

I kicked my shoes off after Nathaniel untied them, ripped off my socks and then pulled Nathaniel up and kissed him.

'I love you so much Nathaniel Coren!'

His lips felt comfortable on mine, but when Nathaniel finished and pulled away, he raised his eyebrow at me and then responded, 'I love you too.' I didn't clear the confusion that he had; a bit of mystery never hurt anybody.

The entire night was amazing. It felt like life was finally coming together for once and I was ready, ready for what I knew was yet to come. I was almost scared, waiting for something to interrupt my karma and make a mess of things. It made me happy to think that we were going to be spending so much more time together, starting with the rest of the weekend, more accurately, the rest of the night.

I woke up the next morning to Nathaniel gently shaking me into consciousness, all I could think was 'why?' His eyes were piercing into me like he was watching into my soul, he smiled at me.

'Good morning baby.'

I couldn't help but smile, still unsure as to why he woke me up.

'Is something wrong? Is it Victoria, is she Okay?!' I was trying to rub the sleep out of my eyes, but I was also worried.

Nathaniel leaned in, giving me a kiss on the forehead.

'Everything is fine, it's just that it's almost 10am and I was getting hungry. I was wondering if you wanted to go get something for breakfast or if you wanted to stay in?'

I wasn't too hungry, but I'd eat either way. 'Up to you, I'm just happy to have breakfast with you.' I winked.

'Cheese ball,' he grabbed the blanket and pulled it back, sending a rush of cold right onto my body. I groaned in discontent. I reached over to grab the covers back, but Nathaniel intercepted my arm, pulled me up and hugged me. In the middle of his hug, I felt him shifting his body weight, moving my body. He flipped me and wrestled me, pinning me down and kissing me while his body was on top of mine. His fingers travelled through my hair and landed on my face as we continued to kiss. Moments later we pulled away, Nathaniel let his hands run across my chest, flowing down my body. He looked up at me, winked.

'Maybe breakfast can wait for a little while,' he said.

By the time we had breakfast it was almost lunch time, and we were both more than ready to eat. We went to a local café and had some croissants and coffee. The sun was out, glistening on our skin, but the wind was still cold. Nathaniel seemed very excited to be relaxing. We were enjoying our time in the sunshine.

Nathaniel asked, 'What would you like to do today?'

Oh God, I hated thinking of things on the spot. I ran my mind through some suggestions to try and think about what to do. The weather at least helped.

'Maybe we should be cute and have a picnic while the sun is out. If you prefer, we could go see a movie instead.' I didn't really mind what we did.

Nathaniel teased, 'Wow you actually have suggestions for once! Why don't we do both?'

And so, we did, we went home after breakfast and we packed food to go and have a picnic. We went to a park that was about 20 minutes away by car. The grass was a little dewy, but I couldn't feel it once we sat over a blanket. We planted ourselves down and got to talking while watching people as they walked by enjoying their day. I'd never actually had a picnic before meeting Nathaniel, I knew it would be something that Nathaniel would be up for. It wasn't as romantic as I thought, but it was still cute. The park was nice and I enjoyed soaking in the sun. Although, a lot of people walking past were staring at Nathaniel and me. Not everyone was used to what they were seeing.

Nathaniel and I didn't stay for too long, maybe an hour and a half or so. I felt bad because it was sort of my idea and I know he usually enjoyed picnics, but I think he preferred organising it himself. We didn't eat too much of the food we packed either because it wasn't too long ago that we'd had breakfast, but we ate enough for the picnic to be worth it, at least I thought so. This is why I don't like making the suggestions.

'Do you still want to go to see a movie?'

Without hesitating, Nathaniel looked at me and responded.

'Yeah of course! Did you have a movie in mind?'

I was surprised that he still wanted to do something, not that I didn't want to see a movie, but I didn't want Nathaniel to be bored.

'I'm not too fussy, you decide what to watch.'

He grabbed out his phone and searched for the session times. He decided that we were watching a movie called 'Fences', I'd seen the trailer for it, and I was happy to watch anything with Viola Davis.

We packed up the blanket and food before we headed straight to the cinema. We got our tickets and even though we were both pretty full, we still got a small bucked of popcorn because how could we not? There were quite a few people in the cinema, but it wasn't full, the movie had been released a couple of weeks back. We had most of the row to ourselves, so we were able to make ourselves comfortable.

The movie was interesting to say the least. It was a little slow to start with, but overall, it was a very captivating and strong movie. Nathaniel had eaten most of the popcorn before the movie finished, and admittedly I helped too. When the movie finished and we made our way out of the cinema, we got some ice cream on the way to the car. Ice cream twice in two days, but who's counting?

We got home and lounged around for the rest of the night. It was exciting to spend the day together the way we did, but it was also a little tiring. Sometimes when you finally get some time to breathe, everything just starts to catch up with you and I think that's what might have been happening. It wasn't even 10:30pm and I was already tired.

We both stayed in bed for a while on Sunday morning. We didn't have much planned for the day, just shopping for some clothes and browsing the department stores. We, of course, needed to have breakfast first so by the time Nathaniel and I got to the mall it was already lunch time. We didn't have too much motivation, just walking around window shopping a little, taking our time enjoying the shops.

Nathaniel's first stop, as usual, was the shoe store. It was always a good sneaker that would catch Nathaniel's eye. He tried on a few pairs and eventually found a nice black and red pair. I almost bought a similar pair, but I didn't really find any that made me want to spend my money. We continued walking around the mall and we ended up checking out a few different men's clothing stores. I needed to get some jeans and a couple of tops too, Nathaniel said he needed some tops also, joking that he could just wear mine.

It was safe to say that we both ended up walking out with a few more items than intended. My stomach made a noise that was louder than it should've been. Even Nathaniel reacted to it, and it was telling me that it was time to eat. Nathaniel agreed and so we went to the food court to get something for lunch. There were quite a lot of people at the mall today, but not enough for it to be too overwhelming, it was actually quite nice and relaxing.

After we finished eating, we spent some more time shopping around the mall. We made it to a bookstore and an electronics store, but we didn't make any purchases. We were already carrying so many bags of shopping, but Nathaniel still wanted to go to a department store and so we did. We went to look around in the home section and Nathaniel smirked at me because he knew that it was one of my weaknesses.

Everything around me was tempting and somehow beautiful. There were some really interesting cushions and then there was more décor in other aisles. There were soap dispensers, candles and tissue box covers to tabletop decorations, placemats and an amazing dinner set. There was also a vibrant ceramic monkey figurine that I really wanted to get. I just loved decorating even if there was no reason to do so. I had to get myself out of the section before I spent even more money. We made our way into the clothes department again, only this time it was the baby's section.

Nathaniel walked towards and grabbed a beautiful looking onesie that had these pretty little frills around the waist.

'Wouldn't this look cute on the baby?' he said.

He turned to me and saw my face drop open, the onesie that Nathaniel picked up and was holding was a dulled down pink. He seemed a little confused at first as to what was happening, but then I think he realised what he had just done because his eyes widened immensely, and he covered his mouth after letting out an audible gasp.

I couldn't move, all I could think was that we were having a girl. I managed to ask him quietly under my breath if we were having a girl.

He nodded in response. I felt goosebumps rise on my skin and the happiness leak from my eyes. Nathaniel put the onesie back on the rack, dropped the shopping bags and came to with his arms opened. He squeezed them tightly around me and caressed the back of my head after wiping the tears from my face. He then started to apologise.

'Jacob, I am so sorry, I didn't even realise what I had done, it was just out of instinct. I'm sorry!'

I could hear the sincerity in Nathaniel's voice. I felt bad that he was feeling guilty, but I was still too much in shock to say anything. I put my arms around Nathaniel, giving him back the warmth that he was giving to me. I asked him again, more out of confirmation.

'So, we are having a girl?'

Nathaniel looked me in the eyes, nodded his head saying yes, then he bit his lip.

'Are you angry at me?' he asked, reluctantly.

I smiled instantly at his question, realising just how guilty he was truly feeling.

'Nathaniel, no! Not at all, it was still some sort of surprise, it just makes me even happier.' I truly meant it too. I leaned back in and hugged Nathaniel again, my cheeks starting to hurt from the smiling.

'I love you.' Nathaniel said, sounding relieved that I wasn't upset with him.

'I love you too.' I replied with a smile.

Nathaniel eyes were giving me a strange look, a stuttering question followed.

'Well, umm, now that you know we are having a girl… can we shop for baby clothes or is it too soon?'

'Why not?' I conceded.

We spent the next hour or so browsing the store and looking at the different clothes for the baby. We tried our best to get a variety of styles as well as a number of sizes, but there was quite a lot of pink and floral. One of the pieces of advice the Mum gave me was not to but too many items of clothing in the same sizes because the baby will grow so fast that most of the clothes won't fit by the time you try them on.

We left the mall with about seven bags of shopping, comprised of clothes both for us and the baby. The drive home was peaceful and all I could think about the entire ride home and for the rest of the day was that we were going to be having a baby girl. That was, until we were interrupted.

Before we made it home to the apartment, Nathaniel got a call from Stefan. While I was driving, Stefan was telling Nathaniel that his mother was currently at the hospital and was already going into labour, and he wasn't sure how long it would take.

We quickly changed directions, rushed ourselves to the hospital as fast as we could without even returning to the apartment.

When we reached the hospital, we quickly found Marissa's room and on entrance we noticed that there was a beautiful newborn baby already resting in his mother's arms. Marissa looked worn out, but she was still radiantly delighted. Stefan and Mitchel both seemed fearful and excited simultaneously.

The baby boy, named Jesse, was almost a week earlier than expected but there weren't any complications or issues with the baby or with Marissa. The entire process was perfect, and the end result was beautiful. There was still almost six weeks until Victoria would be due.

By the time Nathaniel and I got back home to the apartment it was almost one o'clock in the morning. We changed into some more comfortable clothes and fell asleep almost instantly once we climbed under the covers. We didn't even get the shopping out of the car and even through all the commotion, I still couldn't stop thinking about the fact that we were going to be having a girl.

CHAPTER 17

Persistent, Resilient, Eager

Exactly three weeks after Jesse was born, Nathaniel's phone started vibrating, then ringing. My eyes opened slightly, and I grabbed my phone to see that it was 4:44 in the morning before immediately shutting it again. My ears listened to Nathaniel answering his phone. He mumbled to me that it was Victoria's name that was on the screen which made my body shudder out of panic.

'Hello? Victoria, is something wrong?' Nathaniel answered without hesitation.

Greg responded, 'Hey Nathaniel, we just made our way to the hospital because Victoria was having some pains and there might be some complications with the baby. The doctors are running some tests and are going to analyse, there's a possibility that they may need to induce labour early.'

Nathaniel looked at me and said, 'Okay Greg, we'll make our way now, message me the room details and we will see you soon!'

Nathaniel tried to wake me up properly, but I was already awake. We didn't have our hospital bag ready because it was still almost a month early. We swiftly grabbed some things just in case, some nappies even though I don't think we would need them just yet, a bunch of towels and clothes, and then we raced down to the car and then the hospital. The drive to the hospital was extremely terrifying, there wasn't any traffic or anything. The roads were pretty clear at this time of the morning, but Nathaniel was driving a little faster than he should have been, and my heart was pounding. We made it to the hospital in about ten minutes. Normally it would take at least 15 minutes.

On entrance, the hospital was icy cold inside. The air conditioning was definitely on a low temperature because the chills were rising on my arms. We ran to the reception desk and told them the room number that Greg had messaged us. Greg must have let them know to let us into the room. We entered into the room and Victoria was laying on the bed with Greg by her side sitting with her, his hand was moulded into hers. They both looked up at us and smiled, welcoming us in the room. There weren't any doctors around. Greg spoke first when he realised our wandering eyes didn't meet anybody else's.

'The obstetrician ran some scans earlier and is deciding what the best option is.'

Victoria smiled, and made a light groaning noise.

'They want the baby to come out as soon as possible,' she announced. 'I feel it will be okay either way. The obstetrician said that waiting the three weeks would of course be more ideal, but the baby might be ready. My water broke already even though it's early. So, you might be getting the baby a little earlier than you guys anticipated.'

Nathaniel grinned as he moved closer to Victoria, I also moved in and sat next to Greg.

'And how are you feeling Victoria? Are you in a lot of pain?' I asked, worried about what she was going through.

'It all feels a little invasive and it's not the most comfortable position, but it isn't anything that I can't handle.'

Her head shifted as she diverted her attention to Greg, she gave him a look, but he didn't really understand what she wanted so she spoke.

'Greg, can you put the envelope in their bag please? Jacob and Nathaniel, you can't open it now, wait until the time feels right and then open it.' She sounded very cryptic.

Greg put the envelope inside our last-minute baby bag that we brought with us. I looked at Nathaniel and he nodded as if he knew exactly what I was thinking.

'Well, while we're delivering gifts, Nathaniel and I got you both a gift.' Victoria's face contorted in disagreement, but I continued before she could interrupt.

'I know you didn't want money or anything too excessive, so we tried to compromise. It took us a while to finally decide what to get for the both of you, but we decided to purchase a voucher for a week away at a resort and it's only a couple of hours away, it's near the beach and you can decide when you want to go.'

Victoria seemed like she was angry and then without a moment wasted she started tearing up.

'Thank you both so much, you have made this entire process more amazing than I could have expected and I…' she said.

Nathaniel spoke, 'we are the only people who should be thankful for anything right now Victoria, you are giving us the miracle of life, literally. This gesture isn't even slightly enough to say thank you. In fact, we have another thing for you, sort of.'

I spoke to Nathaniel shortly after I learnt that we were going to be having a baby girl. I told Nathaniel when we initially decided on a gift that I had a secret gift in mind. I talked to Nathaniel and I told him what my idea was, and he'd immediately agreed, he thought it was a beautiful idea. The only issue from here on was that we weren't too sure how Victoria would respond. I was going to break the news to her, but Nathaniel did instead.

'We would love for you to be the one to name the baby. We understand that both you and Greg don't want to be too involved with the baby, but the least we could do is ask for you to name the baby.'

Victoria smiled gleefully and looked at us.

'Have you guys got any ideas yet?'

'We do,' Nathaniel and I harmonised before I took the lead. 'However, we don't want to cloud any judgement, this is your decision.'

'All right, do you mind giving Greg and I a minute to discuss this, so we can see what we think.' Surprisingly, Victoria took it quite well, better than I assumed she would.

Both Nathaniel and I stepped out for about five minutes or so before Greg came outside to usher us back in. We walked in, stood in front of Victoria, and waited for her to reveal her thoughts.

'After some thought and discussion, if I can truly name the baby, I think she should be named… Chocolate-Chip.' Victoria deadpanned after she said that.

I could only imagine the face I pulled in response, I felt my eyebrow rise in confusion and I wasn't entirely sure what Nathaniel was thinking but I heard him a long extended 'uhh' escape from his mouth. I wasn't sure if Victoria was being serious or not.

Nathaniel and I looked at each other and tried to telepathically convince each other that the name 'Chocolate-chip' could work. The awkwardness that rose lasted for moments on end. Eventually, Victoria broke the silence by bursting out into laughter while holding her belly.

'The look on both of your faces, oh my goodness!' Greg also started laughing. 'Obviously that's not what I want to name her. In fact, I don't want to be responsible for naming your baby. This is the beginning of your journey, your own little family, for the both of you. We'll be here for as long as we can, but this is the start of your family, which means you should be the ones to name her with whatever name you decide to choose.'

Nathaniel looked at me and saw that I was crying after he heard me sniffling, he came over to me and hugged me. I was just so emotional after Victoria spoke, but I wasn't sure why. It wasn't too long before Nathaniel's eyes mimicked mine.

'You guys are both wrecks, why are you even crying? Nothing sad is happening!' Victoria kept trying to calm us down.

Shortly after we wiped away the tears, the obstetrician walked into the room.

'Oh, hello! You must be the parents?' Nathaniel and I nodded in sync. 'Nice to meet the both of you, I've got some good news. The baby looks as though it's positioned well, it's definitely ready to come out even though it's a little earlier than planned. That would explain the water breaking when it did. We might have to do some exercises to further induce the labour.'

The doctor then turned his head to Victoria before continuing.

'I think you're already aware of what goes on from here. At the moment, your cervix has dilated to roughly two centimetres in diameter. Once it reaches between four to five centimetres, we can give you the epidural. Are your contractions far apart or closer together?'

Victoria looked like she had to think about it for a while.

'I can't really tell, I've had the awkward pains, but I don't know how far apart they are.'

'Okay, well there are several ways to help induce labour, we can either…'

Victoria interrupted before the doctor could continue.

'Yeah, I'll just do some exercise for a bit. I'll walk around but if nothing happens, just give me the Pitocin so we can get it over with.'

We all helped Victoria get up and we spent quite a while walking around the hospital with her. Observing the other patients, we saw that there were two other women doing the same thing. They were waddling around the hospital, very heavy footed, with their partners smiling at us. All four of us took our time walking around the hospital with Victoria, but after a few laps, Greg took a rest and sat inside the room, Nathaniel joined him shortly after.

A couple of hours later, or at least what felt like hours, one of the other women started yelling, from pain or excitement it wasn't clear. She then made her way to her room, as her time to push had arrived. I could tell that Victoria was starting to get impatient and irritated, so I suggested we take a rest, thus we went back into the room and enjoyed the break. Greg decided to go get some food, I went with him to help.

There was quite a wait to get food. By the time we made our way back into the room, the doctor had returned and was assessing Victoria. Victoria's face lit up at the sight of the food, and possibly the smell. According to the doctor, Victoria's cervix was currently expanded to four centimetres in diameter, so it was best to have some food now before the baby started making her way out.

Victoria ate, as we all did, while we watched the doctor. He barely left the room except to start preparations for the birth of the baby. Victoria was still eating even after we'd all finished, after all she was still eating for two.

The doctor called in two nurses once Victoria had finished eating to help prepare Victoria for labour. They inserted the IV drip into her arm for fluids and also had Victoria sit up, so they could inject the epidural. One of the nurses stepped out of the room while the other nurse and doctor continued to prepare.

'The epidural may take a few moments before it shows its effect, but it should alleviate quite a lot of the pain.' The nurse informed us politely, even though we already knew.

A contraction arose, forcing Victoria to contort a little and moan in agony. The doctor asked Victoria to adjust her positioning and then manoeuvred the angle of the bed to check the process.

'The contractions are still irregular. They should occur more consistently, and they might hurt as we get closer to the time.'

Greg, Nathaniel, and I all gathered closer to Victoria, Greg holding her hand waiting for her grip to tighten with pain. The nurse was next to the doctor and a different nurse brought in a tray. It looked as though half of it were wet towels for Victoria, then there were a few other spare towels, some equipment, and a blanket, probably to wrap the baby in once she arrived.

The doctor announced that it was time to push, the baby was ready to come out and Victoria's cervix broadened into a great enough diameter to begin pushing.

'Okay Victoria, we're getting to the home stretch now. It's going to be somewhat intense from here on out.' We all tried to comfort Victoria as much as possible. I grabbed one of the cold towels and had it ready for whenever Victoria wanted it.

'Now is the time for you to start pushing.'

While this might be Victoria's first-time giving birth, she certainly knew what she was doing. The noise that extended from her mouth was aggressive and powerful.

Surprisingly enough, her breathing was controlled. I'm not too sure whether she was in pain, but she very well inflicted some onto the hands of Greg and Nathaniel, judging by their faces and the marks on their hands. Victoria's face was sweating and after a single glance I placed the cold towel immediately onto her forehead.

I was unaware of how long it took, but it felt like at least an hour of constant pushing and breathing before Victoria stopped for a short break. I was on towel duty, regularly rotating a cold towel on her head to help her feel as comfortable as possible. Moments after we began the process again, Victoria made a sound that was like a piercing howl and if the push had any correlation to the scream, then Victoria was pushing a lot harder than when she started.

'The baby is crowning Victoria! You are doing amazingly but you have to continue pushing!' The doctor ordered.

With those orders, Victoria's grip on both Nathaniel and Greg's hands visibly tightened as she readied herself to continue pushing. She inhaled a long, deep breath and exhaled with a strong push, she sustained and maintained this while pushing. Victoria repeated this process over and over for quite some time.

The build-up was intense, Victoria kept on pushing, harder and harder, and the doctor kept talking with Victoria, encouraging her to continue what she was doing because the baby was almost out.

Before we knew it, Victoria gave a drastic, intense, and concluding push and the doctor rose in excitement that the baby was finally out.

Within seconds, the nurse wiped the baby down, wrapped her in the blanket.

'Congratulations, it's a baby girl!' she said. She proceeded to hand the baby over to Victoria and asked if she wanted to cut the umbilical cord. Victoria rejected the offer, and the nurse looked to Greg who also denied the notion, so Nathaniel took the opportunity.

Nathaniel cut the cord and was smiling the entire time while looking at the baby. Our baby. It all seemed so surreal. The nurse then handed the baby over to Victoria, who was reluctant at first, but then carefully held the baby and gave her a peck on the forehead.

'It's time to meet your parents' little girl!' she said. Greg did the honours of taking the baby from Victoria's arms. He looked down at the baby, smiled and kissed the baby on the head before passing her onto Nathaniel.

When Nathaniel was handed the baby, he almost immediately started crying. Nathaniel, not the baby… The baby was also crying but not for the same reason as Nathaniel. Victoria started laughing and Greg started to chuckle. He was talking to her and interacting with her. I was starting to get nervous about holding her myself.

I could feel myself shaking when Nathaniel tried to let me hold the baby, so I took a few deep breaths and let her fall into my arms. Her eyes were still shut but I still looked at them as if they were open. I won't lie, she wasn't the cutest baby ever, but most babies don't look entirely gorgeous at first. However, she was beautiful, especially considering everything she's been through.

My eyes started fogging up from all of the emotions taking over me.

Not too long after, the nurse quickly took the baby for a clean and a routine check-up. This was more vital because the baby was almost three weeks premature.

'How are you feeling Victoria?'

She was lying in the bed, and she looked worn out.

'I'm not in any pain. I'm tired and hungry. I can't believe I just gave birth to the baby though; it's all done and dusted.' An idea came into my head as Victoria spoke. I quickly grabbed my phone and ordered some food, pizza for all of us, but specifically for Victoria.

The nurse came back with the baby. She said that everything was fine, the extra weeks would have been great, but the baby is healthy. The nurse handed over the baby to Nathaniel.

'Thank you for everything.' Nathaniel said to the nurse, 'please pass on my thanks to the doctor as well.'

Greg spoke out and asked, 'Have you guys decided on a name for her yet?'

Truthfully, we hadn't stuck to anything yet, we had a few ideas, but nothing was set in stone except for one name. I gave Nathaniel the look and then he spoke.

'We're still trying to decide what name to go with, for now I think we're going to trial the name… Victoria. What do you guys think?'

Greg was smiling from ear to ear, 'I love it, my favourite name. How beautiful of you guys.' It almost sounded as though Greg was starting to choke up.

I turned to Victoria and she began to cry. She almost started to sob. I walked over and hugged her, holding back my laughter.

'It's the hormones I swear!' She mumbled. She took a moment to calm down, still tearful, and she continued to talk. 'I am grateful, that you want to name her Victoria, but please don't feel obligated to do so. I want you to name her whatever name you'd like to pick.'

Nathaniel tried to defend the name, but I spoke first.

'We didn't like many other names. They didn't fit the way that Victoria does. The name suits perfectly because there's a lot of meaning behind the name. We were going to wait a bit before filling out the forms, but we are completely certain about it.'

Shortly afterwards, the doctor came in for a quick check up before going home. His face lit up at the sight of the baby. Then he turned to Victoria, I think he saw the tears from her eyes and the tiredness on her face.

'How's everything going?'

Victoria spoke and said, 'I feel exhausted and hungry but there's no pain or anything like that.'

'That's good to hear. Well you should try to get some rest and if you need any help just press the button.' He turned his head back out the door and said, 'it looks like you won't be hungry for much longer, your pizza has arrived!'

Victoria sounded heartbroken, 'That sounds perfect; however, we didn't order any pizza though.'

'Actually, I did.' I interjected before Victoria could continue any further. 'I ordered the pizza, pepperoni for you. I owe you one and many many more. There's more than enough for all of us, including you guys.' I looked towards the doctor and nurses. 'Please feel free to join us and have some food, to thank you for everything you've done, it's the least we could do.'

So, they did, we all sat in the room eating pizza. I fed some to Nathaniel while he was holding and cradling baby Victoria, who was sound asleep in his arms. Not too long afterwards, mother Victoria also fell asleep while we all slowly took our moments to eat and relax, each of us resting.

CHAPTER 18

Epilogue: Adjusting

Baby Victoria had only been home with us for a week, but the entire apartment had been turned upside down. It was such a mess, but we were still getting things organised considering baby Victoria had arrived earlier than we'd all expected. Both mine and Nathaniel's family had visited, bringing clothes for the baby and food for us, making sure that we were still keeping ourselves alive just as well as the baby. Victoria met her uncle Jesse, Nathaniel's baby brother, who was less than a month older than her. Nathaniel's mother wanted them to bond with each other as much as possible.

Nathaniel and I were taking turns sleeping and caring for the baby. She was sleeping two to three times a day, which was usually nap time for one of us, sometimes both, or a shower and cleaning time. We were trying our best to maintain a sleeping schedule, but it hadn't been the easiest. This morning, Victoria slept for a solid five hours through the night, which meant we were both able to get a decent sleep. Victoria's cries did wake us up at the crack of dawn, but considering the previous nights, that was a sleep in.

Since neither I or Nathaniel have breasts, we'd been feeding Victoria with baby formula and she seemed to love it. Nathaniel's mother was coming over soon so that we could take the babies for a walk in the stroller. We had barely been out of the house and this will be baby Vickie's first time out since arriving at the house. It was a little early to take her out of the house, some might say, but it wasn't too sunny outside, and we had a shade on the stroller of course. We planned to go a little later anyway, once the sun started going down.

By about 12:30pm, baby Vickie was already falling asleep for another nap. We let her do so. We could wake her up in a couple of hours for a walk and some milk. At that moment, Nathaniel and I both seemed to be wide awake. We took the opportunity to do some cleaning, but the only problem was that we didn't know where to start.

We managed to clean some of the house and we both had a shower, in turns of course. I got in the shower after Nathaniel and thankfully there was still warm water left. When I stepped out of the shower, Nathaniel was sitting on the couch. I was feeling a little frisky and I went over to Nathaniel to try and kiss him, but I realised he had a piece of paper in his hand. I noticed the baby bag that we took to the hospital was on the floor next to him, but baby Vickie was still sleeping.

'What are you reading?' I asked.

The envelope was opened next to him. It must have been the envelope from Victoria, the one Greg had put in our bag. Greg and Victoria were already enjoying themselves on their getaway vacation at the resort. They managed to adjust their schedules immediately and went to enjoy their getaway. Nathaniel didn't really speak; he seemed frozen in his place, except his hand shifted as he passed me the paper. It was a letter…

To Nathaniel and Jacob,

This was the only possible way that I would be able to deliver this information to you. I wanted to do this in person but there is no way that I was going to be able to do that, it made me cringe and feel uncomfortable just at the thought of it.

To start off, I want to say thank you for letting me give you both the opportunity to have this baby for you. I know for a fact that when this baby comes you will be the best parents that you can be.

The reason I'm writing this letter is to tell you the entire truth about my condition. At first, I told you guys that my cancer was at a stage two condition and that I was getting my treatments done. I then told you that I was getting better. Both of these things were a lie. By the time I had told you guys, also around when I learned that I was pregnant, I had been told that I had about a year or so left to live.

I think because of that, I selfishly wanted to have the baby so that I could prove to myself that I could do it and to also know that I left something in this world other than my achievements. Then, when I thought about Greg not wanting a baby, I thought that maybe I could do it as a favour instead, so, I'm glad it all worked out. I wanted to keep working and trying to live life normally, I didn't want any extravagant world travels. The doctors said that the cancer wouldn't spread to the baby and they made sure of that with every check-up.

Thankfully, Greg was on the same page as me and was supportive of everything I was doing and have done so far. I know for a fact that Greg has said he doesn't want kids and doesn't want to raise the baby, but if I can ask you boys for one favour please. Try to include Greg as much as you can with the baby's life and with yourselves. He might not always want to come but invite him over sometimes. He might even want to babysit. Once things have settled down, after I ... go, take him out sometimes and let him enjoy himself, he still needs to live the rest of his life and I want him to be happy.

As for the both of you, I want you to live your lives as best as you can and know that when things get tough, you will always have each other. Once you finish reading this, I know you both are going to try and run to me as fast as possible, but I must ask that you don't do that. Take some time for yourselves to process everything but when we see each other next, I want you to try and act as though everything is normal. You each get one long hug and that's it. Please don't call me right after reading this, everything will be Okay.

From Victoria.

When I finished reading the letter, I felt the warm tears rush down my face as I struggled to catch my breath. I looked over at Nathaniel through my glossy fogged eyes and he was in shock, unable to move. I reached over, pulled him into me and within moments I felt his tears fall onto me as his cries slowly released from his mouth. We dove into each other until we were all out of tears.

One month later, Nathaniel and Jacob were standing a few rows back with baby Victoria asleep in Jacob's arms.

They both stood up, as did everyone, whilst Greg moved in front of the casket as it was being lowered into the grave. Greg ceremoniously picked up a handful of dirt and kissed his hand before releasing it into his wife's grave.

Nathaniel and I held back the tears as they both looked down at baby Victoria.

'You've got a big name to live up to, Vickie.' Nathaniel whispered to her, 'and we're going to love you no matter what.'

At the end of the funeral, they both waited for Greg to be alone and after everybody went home, they asked Greg to come to the pub. He refused at first, but after some insisting, they all went to the pub. They had a beer each and spent some time listening to Greg tell story after story through the tears while Victoria was soundlessly asleep.

Milton Keynes UK
Ingram Content Group UK Ltd.
UKHW030025180324
439604UK00001B/81